The Warm Summer

ZONDERVAN HEARTH BOOKS

Available from your Christian Bookseller

Book Number

Hearth Romances

2	*The Deepening Stream*	Francena Arnold
3	*Fruit for Tomorrow*	Francena Arnold
4	*Light in My Window*	Francena Arnold
5	*The Barrier*	Sallie Lee Bell
6	*By Strange Paths*	Sallie Lee Bell
7	*The Last Surrender*	Sallie Lee Bell
9	*Romance Along the Bayou*	Sallie Lee Bell
10	*The Scar*	Sallie Lee Bell
11	*The Substitute*	Sallie Lee Bell
12	*Through Golden Meadows*	Sallie Lee Bell
13	*Until the Day Break*	Sallie Lee Bell
16	*This Side of Tomorrow*	Ruth Livingston Hill
17	*Give Me Thy Vineyard*	Guy Howard
19	*Judith*	N. I. Saloff-Astakhoff
20	*Trumpets in the Morning*	Lon Woodrum
21	*Light From the Hill*	Sallie Lee Bell
22	*The Bond Slave*	Sallie Lee Bell
27	*The Queen's Jest*	Sallie Lee Bell
28	*Young Man, Young Man*	Eda Stertz
30	*'Til Night Is Gone*	Phyllis Primmer

Hearth Classics

29	*Right On With Love*	Lon Woodrum
31	*The Warm Summer*	Craig Massey

Hearth Mysteries

8	*The Long Search*	Sallie Lee Bell
14	*Candle of the Wicked*	Elizabeth Brown

Sebastian Thrillers

23	*Code Name Sebastian*	James L. Johnson
24	*The Nine Lives of Alphonse*	James L. Johnson
25	*A Handful of Dominoes*	James L. Johnson
26	*A Piece of the Moon is Missing*	James L. Johnson

A HEARTH CLASSIC

The Warm Summer

Craig Massey

ZONDERVAN
PUBLISHING HOUSE

OF THE ZONDERVAN CORPORATION | GRAND RAPIDS, MICHIGAN 49506

Copyright © 1968 by The Moody Bible Institute of Chicago

Assigned to Craig Massey 1980

Hearth Books edition 1980

Second printing 1981

Library of Congress Cataloging in Publication Data

Massey, Craig.
    The warm summer.

    (Hearth series)
    Reprint of the ed. published by the Moody Bible Institute of Chicago.
    SUMMARY: The adventures of a 14-year-old boy during a long hot summer in his small hometown include outwitting the town swindler, going into business with his father, falling in love, and finding God.
    [1. Family life—Fiction]   I. Title.
[PZ7.M4238War 1980]   [Fic]   79-24210
ISBN 0-310-41772-4

Printed in the United States of America

Library of Congress Catalog Card Number 68-18885

Dedicated to
ROGER,
my son.
May his memories of boyhood
be as
pleasant as mine.

CHAPTER 1

I KICKED MY BLANKET to the bottom of the bed. I wiggled around so my head was near the open window. The breeze billowed the curtains like cheeks full of air, until they parted in the middle and fell back in place. The air swept over my face, my shoulders, and worked its way down my back and legs. It built up as nice a case of gooseflesh as a body would be likely to find anywhere.

I rolled over and the gooseflesh simmered down. The curtains puffed again, but that breeze was so tender it had to try three times before it curled them open. Another case of gooseflesh developed but it wasn't near as satisfying as the first.

I sucked in my breath, trying to untangle the smells the morning air carried, and it carried a heap of them. The breeze had moved over fields, woods and along Canoe Brook. It had visited the barn, the pigpen, the hen house and Mama's petunia patch. A chunk of it must have come through the kitchen door and up the stairs, for a smell of coffee hung on it. It was downright comforting for a fellow to wake up to a thing like that.

I studied a patch of sunlight on the wall and was bothered some by the number of fingerprints I spotted. I was bothered a little more by the amount of dust on the shelves holding my bird's nest and rock collections. I was glad Mama hadn't seen those things.

I was a heap gladder my sister Lillie hadn't seen those things. Lillie was bossier than Mama and louder, and she could nag at a thing until you could almost taste it. Lillie was bossier and brassier than Arnie Beard, and that would make her about the hardest person in the world to get along with, and she was.

I couldn't count the times she had marched into my room and climbed all over me for what she saw. Anybody as clean and neat as she was was impractical. I had told her so, too, likely up to a thousand times or more, but she wouldn't listen. She was a terror on dirt generally, but she was a specialist when it came to me. I'd be in the middle of working in the barn, or hoeing corn in the garden patch, and *bang*, she'd show up and order me to clean myself up. Mama would stick up for me heaps of times, but Lillie was so unreasonable she'd come right back at me first time she got a chance.

I laughed out loud when I saw my shirt, pants, socks and shoes lying on the floor between the door and my bed. That would've torn up Lillie considerably. I almost hoped she'd come in, but I knew it was too early for that.

I lazed around for a couple more minutes thinking of what I was going to do for the day. It was Monday. That meant I didn't have to work at Arnie Beard's General Store, since it was my day off. I thought of going over and asking Joe McCormick to go fishing at Kordick's pond. I thought of taking Rusty and going on a woodchuck hunt. I thought of going over the ridge to Indian Valley to hunt for arrowheads. I thought of a lot of other things, but nothing seemed as good as just sprawling on the bed, and that's all I did for about ten minutes.

Mama's voice drifted upstairs. She used the kind of a tone that was loud enough for me to hear if I were awake, but soft enough so as not to disturb anyone who was asleep. That was surprising on a Monday, for Mama's voice usually had a way of waking you up and making you move; not brassy like Lillie's, but forceful.

"Coming," I called softly.

My feet hit the cool floor. I picked up my Sunday clothes and put them away, lulled on a pair of overalls and padded down the hall in my bare feet.

Right off I saw why Mama was so gentle.

Papa was home. His shoes were placed neatly by the bedroom door. It was always like that. I mean, when Papa came home late he always took off his shoes on the back porch and carried them upstairs so he wouldn't wake the family. Papa wasn't supposed to be home. He was supposed to be in Hartford, Connecticut, on a business trip. But he was home all right. Anyone could have known that even without the shooes, for nobody whooped it up like Papa when he snored.

That was music to me. I stepped into the bedroom to see him. His suitcase was open on the floor at the foot of the bed. Dirty clothes were heaped in a pile to the left and the clean clothes were in a neat pile to the right. That was Mama's doing. As soon as breakfast was finished she'd be flailing away at those dirty clothes, getting them ready for Papa's next trip.

I moved to the side of the bed and studied Papa. I seldom saw him as he was at that moment. He was usually the first one up in the morning when he was home. He was usually dressed as neat as a bank president. He wasn't neat now. His mouth was open. He needed a shave. His hair needed combing. His pajama jacket lacked a top button. That had happened somewhere on his last trip, for Mama was one to sew buttons where they were needed. Papa looked generally worn out and run down.

I knew what Papa had done when he had arrived home some time during the night. He had come into my room. He'd run his hand through my hair and probably whispered, "Good ol' Jerry," or, "Hello, son," or some other thing I really couldn't tie into or understand, like, "I hope you make it, boy," or, "I hope you have the stuffin' to lick 'em," or, "I hope you have more of the stuff she's made of than what I am." I knew he said things like those, because heaps of times I had played possum and made believe I was asleep when he came in. He would do it every time. I liked it.

I leaned over and barely touched the hair that had fallen

over his forehead. His hand brushed the spot. I tried again and the same thing happened.

I would've done it again but Mama called, "Jerry, are you coming?"

I left the bedroom and headed down the hall. Betsy bounded from her room dressed in one of Lillie's far-too-big yellow nightgowns. "Boo!" she shrieked.

I caught her up, cradled her in my arms and buried my lips in her wild, yellow hair and whispered, "Hush up, Betsy, hush up. Papa's home."

Her expression changed. She suddenly looked outwardly as I felt inwardly. I carried her downstairs and put her in her high chair at the kitchen table. Mama was at the stove tending a batch of hot cakes.

"Surprise, Mama, surprise, Mama, Papa's home! Papa's home!"

"Yes, Betsy, I know." Mama was different when Papa was home. I couldn't exactly put my finger on it, but she was softer, or more comfortable, or something.

Mama went on, "Papa came home about midnight. He drove all of yesterday to get here." Mama looked at me. "Jerry, you'd best get your milking done so you can spend a little time with your father."

I took the pail from its hook by the door and headed for the barn. Bob the Cat came bounding from among Mama's Sweet Williams. What a show he put on; meowing friendly, weaving between my legs purring and arching his back with his tail straight up as a column of smoke in still air. I wasn't taken in, for the only time Bob the Cat showed any interest in anybody was when he wanted something. Any other time he was as indifferent as a chunk of ice and about as loving. Rusty, on the other hand, though he was nothing but a mixture of most every kind of dog in town, was always ready to dig in and make you feel good. He came from the barn with a considerable amount of tail wagging, hand licking, jumping and barking. You could always count on him doing that any time you were out of his sight more than a few minutes. I liked Rusty.

I knelt down and let my fingers trace the white patches scattered along his bristly brown back. Bob the Cat didn't appreciate the situation. He unsheathed his claws and kneaded my leg; not hard enough to break the skin, but hard enough to let me know he wanted his morning milk.

I gave up fooling with Rusty, not because of Bob the Cat's insistence, but because of Papa, and headed toward the pasture gate. I dropped the bars and Daisy followed me into the barn. Daisy, in her dumb way, was a lot nicer than Bob the Cat. She was half Jersey and half Guernsey and there never was a cow that could produce orange cream like she did. We always had a list of people wanting to buy milk from us.

When I finished milking I fed the three pigs and poured cracked corn in the chicken yard. Bob the Cat tagged after me, tormenting all the time, but as always I made him wait until every other animal was fed before I buckled in to his wants.

I was straining the milk into pans on the kitchen sink a little later when Papa came downstairs. He did not look like the same man I'd seen in bed a little while before. He grabbed Betsy and set her on a giggling streak by kissing her neck. He finally put her back in her chair and shook hands with me.

"Hi, Jerry!"

"Hello, Papa. How long you going to be home?" I asked.

Papa frowned, "You've robbed me of a golden moment, Jerry. I'd clean forgotten duty and responsibility. You've reminded me. I'm not going to be home long."

He went over to Mama and kissed her ear. "You must be expecting somebody very important, Mrs. Ross. That's an elegant lot of pancakes you've whipped up."

Mama smiled and I can't tell you all that was in that smile. "Yes, sir," she said. "I'm expecting a very important man, a nice man."

"Humph," Papa said, making believe he was jealous.

"And he likes pancakes," Mama went on. "He has three children. He doesn't come around here near as often as I would like him to."

11

"Humph," Papa said again.

Mama went on, "He's about six feet tall, and drives a new Model T Ford."

"What's his name?" Papa kept the game going. "And if I meet up with him I'll gladly shoot him."

"His name?" Mama said thoughtfully. "His name is Adam Ross."

Betsy ended the game. "That's him, Mama. That's him. That's Papa. That's Mr. Ross!"

Mama placed a platter of pancakes in the center of the table. "Well, Betsy, what do you know? It is." Mama tiptoed and kissed Papa.

Lillie marched into the kitchen and took over the conversation. She was like a black cloud on a sunny day. "Papa!" she squeaked. "I'm so glad you're home."

Papa looked up at Lillie and announced, "A breath of spring sunshine has arrived," and he meant it, and I couldn't see how he could mean it, but he did. A body could tell the way Papa kissed Lillie, soft and tender, that he meant it.

"Papa, if I'm to have my dress ready for the wedding I simply must have the ribbon today."

"Ribbon?" Papa questioned as he sat at the table.

"The pattern calls for bows of ribbon on the sleeves and at the neck." Lillie explained with an impatient kind of patience that made a body think she was talking to a little boy.

"Doesn't Arnie have ribbon?"

"Arnie? Yes, he has ribbon." It was surprising to see how much edge that girl could get into her voice when she wanted to. "Arnie has pink ribbon and blue ribbon and green ribbon and black ribbon, and every other color ribbon. Indeed, Arnie has ribbon. He has had ribbon for over fifty years. A person who would buy ribbon from Arnie would have to take the yellow ribbon and the black ribbon out into the sunlight to find out which was which, they're that faded and dirty."

Mama sat down and poured coffee. "I can't understand why you didn't order it from the catalog, Lillie. You would have saved a lot of bother."

"Oh, Mama, you don't understand! When a girl is making her own wedding dress she doesn't want mail-order ribbon." She added quickly, "Oh, Mama, I know, you bought everything for your wedding from the catalog, but that was years ago. Things are different now."

Papa sighed good-naturedly. "It sure suited me, Lillie, but maybe I can help you out. I'll be going through New York City. I could stop off at Macy's and get what you want and mail it to you. I should think a lick of Macy's at the wedding would add plenty of prestige and class."

That wasn't what Lillie wanted. "I can't wait that long, Papa. My whole schedule will be thrown off. I need ribbon now—today."

Papa sighed again with a soft patience he always had with Lillie. "I have an idea I shouldn't ask this next question, but Lillie, what is your solution to this problem?"

Lillie had the solution, all right. "If I hurried, I could catch the bus this morning and go to Newark and buy it at Bamberger's."

Papa sighed again, "I rather imagine you'd like me to finance this trip?"

"Oh, Papa, you're wonderful! You're sweet! You're all any girl could ask for in a father!" Lillie leaped from her chair, sat on Papa's lap and kissed him.

I was plain disgusted seeing that girl wiggle into getting what she wanted. She was always like that with Papa. At one time she had done the same thing with me, too. But I was little then, and I soon caught on.

If Lillie was bad carrying on with Papa she was a heap worse with Roger. How she'd lead him on to get her way every time! I had pointed this out to Roger a heap of times but he just couldn't see it. It was funny considering how bright he was about other things, but when it came to wanting to marry that girl he just wasn't practical. I figured someday he'd find out and come cowtailing to me telling me I was right all along and how he should've listened.

Lillie was in high gear now. "Papa, while I'm in Newark I might as well buy my shoes." She turned to me and

13

right off I knew I was in for some bossing. "Jerry, it's not too soon for you to gather the kerosene lanterns I want to use for the reception."

Lillie had reminded me about that job at least once a day.

"I want you to visit every house around here," her voice was whispery. "I want our lawn to be so bright and gay that night. I want lanterns in very tree and on the porch railing. I want lanterns over every flower bed."

"Check the calendar, Lillie. Maybe the moon will be out," I said hopefully.

"Moon or no moon, I want lanterns. I figure I'll need at least seventy-five."

"Let's figure I'll get one lantern to a house," I calculated. "That means I'll have to visit seventy-five houses and there ain't that many houses in town."

"There aren't that many houses in town," Lillie snapped.

"Ah, so you admit it yourself. It can't be done. There's no use trying."

"Jerry," Mama interrupted with a warning note, "you do the best you can."

"Papa," Lillie was at it again, "I should get the material for the sash while I'm in town."

"I'm sure glad people around here don't get married every day," I said to my pancake, but loud enough for anybody else to hear if they cared to.

Lillie flashed me a look but Papa was pulling out his wallet so she forgot all about me.

"Lillie, how much do you figure this will cost?"

"Well," Lillie murmured, "there's the ribbon, the shoes, the stockings, the material for my veil—"

There wasn't any point in my staying around any longer, so I gulped the rest of my pancake and went outside. I gathered the eggs and cleaned out the barn. I had tossed a stick for Rusty to fetch about a hundred times when the screen door opened and slammed shut.

Papa came down the porch steps carrying two suitcases.

He walked slowly toward me. I hated those suitcases. I hadn't expected Papa to be hitting the road so soon. The suitcases were made by the same company, of the same kind of leather and were the same shape and size, but they were different. The old, scuffed-up suitcase held Papa's personal things, along with a number of books he would be reading in hotel rooms.

The new suitcase carried the samples of clothes his firm offered for sale: overalls, dungarees, men's underwear, socks and work shirts. Tucked in a separate compartment were the catalogs showing various lines of work shoes, belts, gloves, hats and safety helmets. Along with the catalogs were order blanks.

The suitcases and Papa belonged to one another. I watched him walk across the sunny lawn. Suddenly I hated him as much as I hated the suitcases. Who was he anyway—a stranger? Everybody said he was away too much. Where was he when Mama cried when Betsy had the high fever? Papa hadn't taken three steps before guilt hit me. It left me limp and choked up.

"Well, Jerry, I'm off again," Papa said.

He placed the suitcases on the cement floor and slid them forward a couple of feet with just the right speed and pitch to make them come together so neatly you would think a body took five minutes to match them up. I had tried that trick myself. It never worked for me. That's one thing I could say for Papa; he had had a heap of experience with suitcases. He had lived out of them five days a week for over twenty years. Mama told me Papa was in Stroudsburg, Pennsylvania, the day I was born. It wasn't until two days later he knew I had come along.

"I'm off again, Jerry," Papa repeated.

"Uh huh." What else could I say?

"You'll be head of the house until Friday night." He sat on a bale of hay, snapped off a strand and stuck it between his teeth. "I'm taking on a new line of clothes, Jerry." Papa took off his hat and dangled it between his knees, swinging it back and forth. He watched the barn swallows moving in and out the doorway. "A quality line of work clothes."

"Uh huh."

I think Papa forgot I was there. "Business isn't good. Most people have trouble keeping themselves in cheap clothes. Merchants will balk. Well, I'll tell them, buy a better grade. Clothes will last longer. Buy quality. Save money. Buy a reliable name brand—good guarantee. That's what I'll tell them."

Lots of times when Papa was home he'd go over his sales talk. When I was smaller, I figured merchants were grotesque monsters the way Papa talked about them: men who put their hands on their hips, men who stared down at him, men with gaping mouths, men with brassy voices. If they gave an order they wouldn't pay for it. When they got the goods they claimed they were short items. When they received the bills they threw them into the wastebasket.

That childish picture leaped into my mind as I idly swept the broom back and forth and watched Papa. I could see Papa pushing through a door, shy and cringing, expecting a tirade of abuse. I laughed out loud. That picture wasn't true. Papa was a good salesman. Nobody loomed over him. Papa had won a weekend at New York City the year before for being the best salesman. Mama went with Papa, and I know Mama thought Papa was the best salesman in the whole world.

I laughed again. Papa looked at me in a funny way. "What are you laughing at?"

Papa laughed without waiting for an answer. "Take my advice, Jerry, don't plan to be a salesman."

"I'm going to be a farmer. I'm going to take over this old place."

Papa frowned, "Well, just so long as you aren't a salesman. I ought to take you with me, Jerry, that's what I ought to do. That would cure you proper. Let you get a taste of the thing, sleeping in a small-town hotel, eating greasy food, fried in a greasy pan, dumped on a greasy plate, slid in front of you over a greasy counter by a pair of greasy hands."

16

"I'd like that," I said, which didn't make much sense, but I wasn't thinking of the food, I was thinking of the trip.

Papa didn't notice though. He kept swinging his hat back and forth. He seemed to be studying Mama's petunia patch. "And I have a family, but I don't have them. I have a wife and I see her less than one day out of three. I have a daughter who's going to get married and I barely know the boy. I have a four-year-old girl who's growing so fast she changes every time I see her; grows in jumps, not slow and steady-like. I have a son, almost fifteen, who I ought to take on a fishing trip—" He paused and looked at me. "Say, Jerry, I forgot, I haven't been paying you lately. How much do I owe you?"

"Fifty cents a week for barn chores." I had in mind to say I only had a couple weeks' wages coming to me, but I couldn't fool Papa so I went on, "And fifty cents a week for delivering eggs and milk. That's a dollar a week. I figure this is the fourteenth week."

Papa sighed, "That much, huh? Lillie's wedding plans to be a buster, doesn't it? Well, Jerry, you keep track of how much I owe you and after the wedding I'll straighten it up with you." He brightened, "Hey, Jerry, let's knock off next Saturday afternoon. We'll get a little fishing done."

Papa should have remembered I worked for Arnie every Saturday. I said so in a tone of voice that let him know he should have remembered. "You know I work Saturdays."

Papa stared at me. "Aw, Jerry, I'm sorry. I should have remembered. It seems we never make it together, do we, son? Well, I may not get home in time, anyway."

"It's all right, Papa," I said.

"You're a good boy, Jerry." He stood up, put his hat on, brushed the hay from his trousers, shook hands and said, "Good-bye. Take good care of your mother."

But he didn't go. He looked out the barn door at Daisy in the pasture, at the pigpen and the chicken coop. He leaned over and scratched Rusty behind the ears.

The kitchen door squealed and banged. Lillie's voice burst upon us, "I'm ready, Papa."

Papa jerked up and went for his suitcases. "Lillie talked me into driving her down to Newark."

"Papa, I'm ready," Lillie called again.

"So long, Jerry."

"Good-bye, Papa." It's funny how watery a fellow's voice can get sometimes.

Papa hefted the suitcases and headed for the garage. His shoulders were sloped, his head bowed forward ever so little. His coat hung loosely. His pants reflected the sunlight with a dull, metallic glow.

Papa backed the car out of the garage and Mama and Betsy came from the house. Mama held Betsy up to kiss Papa and Mama gave Papa a kiss, just a little one, and I knew somewhere in the house there had been a real one instead of a no-account one like that.

Lillie wiggled into the car and fussed with her hair. Papa sat, not saying anything and not moving; he just sat looking at us.

Lillie finally said, "Papa, if we don't get down there I won't have time to get my shopping done."

That did it. That broke the spell and Papa backed out and with a considerable amount of waving, drove away. Mama and Betsy returned to the house. I went to the barn.

"Good-bye, Papa. Good-bye, Papa." I kicked a bale of hay which turned out to be a foolish thing to do, considering I was barefoot, and considering the bale weighed over a hundred pounds. I yelped, sat down and favored my toe. Rusty came into the barn and licked my toe. That cheered me a bit, but not much.

The mailman was about due and I loafed my way out to the mailbox to wait for him, for Mama was always getting flower catalogs and Papa was always getting clothes catalogs. They were always fun to look at when there was nothing else to do. Right now it seemed like nothing in the world was worth doing.

I heard a truck coming. It wasn't the mailman. It was John Kordick. I could tell that with my eyes shut, for no truck in the whole world carried on the way that one did. I started to duck for some bushes, not wishing to see John, and especially not wishing for him to see me. I was too late. John jammed on the brakes and the truck rolled about one hundred fifty feet before it stopped with a considerably noisy backfire. There was no hood over the motor and the truck was loaded with crates of chickens.

John was a swapper, a trader, a buyer and a seller, and about twice a week he went to the market in Newark with a load of something.

John hefted his weight out of the truck. "You," he called, "come here! Where's yer old man?"

"On a business trip," I replied, keeping a safe distance between us.

John took a dirty match from the corner of his mouth and splashed a mouthful of tobacco juice on the ground. "I wanna see him. I'm gonna tell him you need a whopping—a good one. You've been fishin' at the pond again, ain't ya?"

"No, sir," I fibbed, for I had been fishing there the week before.

"Yer lyin'. I seen ya."

That could have been true because I remembered hearing the truck coming. I had ducked and figured I was out of sight.

John splashed another wad of tobacco juice about a foot from my bare feet. "I been lettin' you get away with fishin' there. I shoulda had you arrested long ago. But I'm warnin' ya now. Things is different. That there pond is gonna be different, too, and I'm warnin' ya, don't you go near that pond again."

Another swirl of tobacco juice splashed in the dust about six inches from my right foot. It's hard to say how I felt when some touched my leg. I felt dirty all over. I could barely wait to wash it off.

John stuck the matchstick in the corner of his mouth, climbed into the truck and drove off.

The mailman's car came into view, so as much as I wanted to go to the brook and wash my leg, I waited. I should have gone to the brook right away. He passed right by with a wave.

CHAPTER 2

I RACED FOR THE BROOK. There were three splashes of brown stain on my foot and ankle. I guess I washed those spots fifty times each, and while the stain was gone the feeling wasn't. So I climbed up on a fallen tree and let my feet dangle in the water and thought of a number of ways to get back at Kordick. But none of them was practical.

I gave up, but still feeling dirty, I walked toward the barn.

I went to the feed barrel and dug under the oats and fetched out my slingshot. Mama was death on slingshots and unreasonable, too, so I tucked it inside my shirt. When I say Mama was death on slingshots, I mean it. Once she was so stirred she started a furnace fire in the middle of August.

It had been the morning of the flower show down in the basement of the church. Mama had built a pretty good reputation for flower arrangements, taking first place seven years in a row. She had spent that entire morning fixing her entry. She had forget-me-nots, pom-pom zinnias, and other flowers in a silvery glass bowl which she had bought for the occasion. It was pretty and would've won hands down, but Mama made a mistake.

She finished the job and set it on a bench near the barn. It was a cool place, shaded by an apple tree and Mama figured it would keep the flowers fresh until time to take it up to the church.

I didn't know that then. I had been practicing with my slingshot in the woods. I was on my way home for lunch. I was pushing through the brush when I spotted a silvery thing that looked like nothing but a tin can between the leaves. I aimed through a gap and let fly. I'll say this, it was a good shot, but my ears told me it wasn't a can. My ears were right. Cans don't fall apart with a glassy, tinkling sound.

I walked up and saw an awful mess of water, glass and flowers.

There was nothing much I could do, so I did nothing, not even bothering to tell Mama.

Along about 1:30 Mama was spruced up and ready to go. You might guess I was concerned when I saw her heading for the flowers, and even more concerned when I heard her scream, and still more concerned when she called, "Jerome Bellamy Ross!"

I walked around the barn innocent and easylike. "Oh, Mama!" I said, looking at the broken glass and heap of flowers. "Who did that?"

Mama was blazing. "Is this your doing, Jerome Bellamy Ross?"

"No, Mama."

"Who then?"

That was a hard question but I came up with an answer, "Bob the Cat, probably."

Mama leaned over and with her thumb and forefinger delicately picked the stone from the middle of the destruction. She placed it on a dry spot on the bench. She turned slowly.

That shows what kind of a fool I was, not thinking to get that stone out of there when I had the chance, but it was too late, and Mama gave me a lick across the cheek that was a real stinger.

"I want your slingshot," she said. "Then you march up to bed. You are going to stay there until tomorrow morning. No supper, either."

So she built the fire, tossed the slingshot in and sent the heat up in the house until it was so blistering hot I figured the temperature in my room went to 140 degrees.

So that's why I tucked the sling inside my shirt now.

Our house was an old one and had been in our family for more than one hundred fifty years, and Papa was proud of it. He always mellowed when he talked about it. "This place was built for the ages. They don't construct homes today the way they used to."

I figured he was right, for the beams in our house were four to six times bigger than the beams in any new house I had ever seen built. The basement walls were of stone and were over two feet thick. Someone had spent a lot of time chipping them to fit one another and they were mortared together with soft, white lime composition. A body could hunt all over and never find so much as a crack. And up in the attic you could see where the beams were held together by oak pegs.

The house had a pillared porch running across the front with another porch running halfway across the back. The back porch was convenient. I could step out of my window onto the roof and climb down the Wisteria trellis without anybody knowing. I had done that a heap of times and nobody ever caught on. Sometimes I'd skin out for a reason, like night fishing with Joe or Halloweening for mischief or for a coon or possum hunt.

There were times, though, I skinned down without any reason at all, maybe just to pet Rusty or watch the rabbits playing on our front lawn in the moonlight, or maybe just to walk around in my bare feet. I figured nobody would understand why I did these things, so I never bothered telling them.

My grandparents and their kinfolk before them farmed the hundred and fifty acres, but when it came to Papa that ended the farming, except for the forty acres we rented to McCormicks for corn or wheat every year.

"I wasn't cut out for farming," Papa said once. "I had a taste of it when I was a tad like you. There was always too much work to do; upwards of thirty cows to milk, barn to clean, corn to hoe, hay to rake, and what did you have when you were finished? I remember one year your grandfather heard beans were going to be scarce so we planted beans; nothing else but beans, beans, beans, beans. Nothing went right that summer, no rain, powder dry. Beetles came, beans

22

went. I don't suppose we harvested fifty bushels and that's what we ate that winter. To this day I'm not a bean eater."

Papa didn't discourage me though. I figured on being a farmer anyway. Daisy was mine, and so were the pigs. Each year I cut enough hay for the winter and grew enough corn for the pigs. To me it was an awful good feeling to see that haymow full and the corncrib with enough in it, but it just didn't strike Papa that way.

There was something else about our house being old that was special. It was Mama's doing. Outside of the family, flowers were her favorite things. Mama was a swapper and she'd swap with anybody, bulb for bulb, seed for seed, root for root, slip for slip. We had color from the crocuses in the spring to the mums after frost.

"Amy," Papa said, "Mrs. McCormick told me you had a green thumb. I told her you had a green heart and a green soul."

One thing for sure, by a big heap it was the prettiest place in town. The house was on a slight knoll with the lawn saucering down in front and going upward in all directions. Woods were on the north side: oak, elm, maple and a few pines. The barn and garden lay to the east behind the house and out of sight more or less. Canoe Brook trickled and pooled on the south edge of our property. The road, of course, flanked the western side.

It was at the bottom of the saucered lawn where Mom worked most with a rock garden and a fishpond and flower patches helter-skelter, but orderly.

The brook side was my favorite, for Mama had over thirty shades of lilac bushes planted there. That was a jungle so thick a body could hide in a dozen places and not be spotted.

I headed for there now, after scooping up a handful of crushed stone from the driveway. I had work to do, but I didn't do it and didn't intend to.

I found a place by the brook and sat down and dangled my feet, still remembering Kordick's tobacco juice. I let my miseries run free.

Bob the Cat caught my eye; a-slithering and a-slinking along the ground like a short-legged orange snake.

A robin—young, speckle-breasted and ignorant—hopped amid the lilacs. I tolerated cats, and I liked birds, but they don't mix. I figured on teaching Bob the Cat a lesson.

I cradled a stone in the slingshot, aimed about four inches in front of the cat's nose and let fly. Dirt exploded. So did Bob the Cat. He flew two feet in the air, landed running and disappeared.

The robin, clumsy and inexperienced, flew to a lilac bush.

I cradled another stone and aimed at the branch he sat on, figuring to educate him and make him afraid of cats and people.

You would think a body would be brighter than I was. I pulled back, aimed and let sail.

That was a mistake and I knew it.

I knew it before the stone went five inches, but there was no way of calling it back and there was no way of moving the attic window as it reflected the sun.

The stone missed the branch but it didn't miss the window. The glass collapsed with a considerable amount of noise.

It's a curious thing to hear silence the way you do sometimes. Everything seemed to stop suddenly; the breeze, the insects, the birds, and even the brook seemed to mute their sounds. It was like I was being watched to see what was going to happen to me.

It happened quick enough. The kitchen door opened and banged shut. The screen door on the porch squealed open and banged shut.

"Jerome Bellamy Ross!"

Run—keep silent—throw the slingshot in the brook—blame a bird for slamming into the window. None of these things would stand up in front of Mama so I gave up and called, "Coming!"

Mama was at the bottom of the porch steps with Betsy. That snip of a girl wasn't helping a bit. "Jerry's bad again!

24

Jerry's bad again! Jerry's bad again!'' She almost sang the words. I calculated she was going to grow up to be like Lillie. I planned to tell her so the first chance I got alone with her.

"Jerome Bellamy Ross, march into that kitchen!"

Mama snatched the slingshot as I went by and followed me inside.

"Jerry, Jerry, why? Why again?

How do you answer a question like that?

"Windows cost money."

"Yes, Mama."

"Yes, Mama? Is that all you can say?"

"Yes, Mama. I mean, I'm sorry, Mama."

I figured I'd get it, but that shows how little I know about things. Mama looked at me for a full minute. Tears pooled up in the corner of her eyes. The next thing I knew she was hugging me, patting my head, kissing me, and murmuring, "Jerry, Jerry, whatever am I going to do with you?"

There were tears in my eyes, too. Don't ask me why, but they were there.

I was taller than Mama and brushed them off in her hair before she let me loose.

It was all over in a minute and Mama was patting her hair back in place and wiping her eyes on her apron. "Lunch is about ready, young man. After we finish eating you fix that window."

That lunch was real enjoyable, quiet-like without Lillie, and somehow I felt better. "I'll have that window fixed in a jiffy, Mama, don't fret yourself."

Fixing the window wasn't much of a job for there were tools and panes of glass in the barn. When I finished I came downstairs, carrying the tools under my arm.

Mama reached out and put her hand on my shoulder. "Jerry, when Papa's gone I depend on you to be the man of the house. You do wonderfully well most of the time."

She went over to the sink and took the slingshot from the windowsill and handed it to me. "I can't take this away from the man of the house, but I could ask him to please be careful from now on."

I wanted to say something, something that would make Mama know she'd never have to worry about me making another mistake with that slingshot but I couldn't think of a thing, so I murmured, "Thank you," and stuck it into my hip pocket and headed for the barn with the tools.

I was cheered by now and figured it was as good a time as any to go over to Joe's and ask him to go fishing. John Kordick was off to market, he'd not plague us, and I had a small satisfaction planning to do something he didn't want me to do.

Rusty caught up with me before I reached the woods and we walked along the path together, him sniffing where squirrels and rabbits had been, and me getting mellower with every step.

I spotted Joe hoeing corn in the garden patch to the south of his house. "Hey, Joe, how about goin' fishin'?" I called from the shade.

Joe didn't look up. He mumbled, barely loud enough for me to hear, "Ain't goin'."

"Aw, come on, why not?"

Joe straightened up, leaned on the hoe, glanced at the barn and suddenly bent to his work again. "I told ya, I ain't goin'," he said in a crotchety way.

It puzzled me some, for Joe wasn't generally like that. I should've had better sense than to hang around to see if he would explain things or change his mind, but I didn't.

I found a shady spot on the stone fence and sat down to wait for developments. It wasn't a long wait.

George Hostler, McCormick's hired man, came barreling out of the barn with a pitchfork in his hand. He was a wiry, half-pint, middle-aged man with a shingle face and enormous ears. I'd never warmed to him and didn't intend to.

He bellowed, and when I thought about it I couldn't remember a time when George spoke without bellowing. "You, Joe, get movin' or I'll lay into you with a hunk of firewood! I'da had that whole patch hoed by this time."

That was another thing about George, he had a way of running everybody down except himself.

"Who was you talkin' to? I heard ya," he stormed, walking toward Joe with the pitchfork jabbing the air.

Joe barely glanced my way but George caught it and whirled toward me with the pitchfork poised. "What are you doin' here?" His voice rose about four notches. "You leave Joe alone. Get out of here! If I was your old man I'd stay home and learn you what a day's work was. Sneaky, good for nothin', loafin' kid, get!"

I got, with Rusty at my heels, growling deep in his throat. I ducked behind some heavy brush and looked back. George turned on Joe. "Don't you get no ideas about sneakin' off with that good for nothin'. Iff'n you do I'll whomp the tar out of you."

Joe boiled, "You lay one finger on me and Ma'll have you off this place in no time."

George made a nasty sound. "Your pa gave me orders to see that you was kept workin'. Iff'n it takes a shingle lickin' to get the work out of you, I'll do it." He jabbed the pitchfork in the ground and leaned on it. "That Jerry's as shifty and lazy as his old man. He'll probably grow up dodgin' work just like his old man does."

About then, if I had been big enough, I'd have gone after George not only for saying that, but saying a heap of other things at other times.

I walked home, trying to think of some way to get back at George, but wasn't too successful.

I didn't figure on wasting my day so I pushed John Kordick and George Hostler out of my mind, but that didn't mean I'd forgotten thinking about how to get back at George. I dug worms, picked up my fishing pole and headed for Kordick's pond. Fishing, I knew, wouldn't be good in the heat of the afternoon, and it was hot, but Kordick's pond was a place to be, even when the fishing was bad.

My path led along Canoe Brook, not at all direct, for it curled through the woods any way it wanted to, not being in any hurry to get anywhere.

Rusty tagged along and about halfway there he stopped and listened. My ears picked up a sound a moment later; the sound of a saw ripping through wood and the sound of a hammer.

This was surprising, for there were no houses nearby and the only building within a mile of the pond was an abandoned mill made of stone by the dam. It was a surprising thing, too, because I figured John was at the Newark Market.

I hooked a finger in Rusty's collar and walked forward with double caution. I worked my way up to the crest of a low ridge and peeked through the brush. The pond, off to my left, lay like a looking glass, reflecting the grove of pines and oaks on the far side. The meadow between the water and me was speckled with clusters of daisies and small cedar trees.

I was in for a surprise. The old mill didn't look like an old mill any longer. The sagging roof had been ripped off and replaced with a new one. Where before there had been only two windows in the three-feet-thick stone walls, there were now twelve, and every one of them twice as big as the originals. A carpenter was working on window frames. Two more were working on a new porch along the front facing the pond.

My grandfather had told me before he died that as a boy he and his father had brought wagonloads of wheat and corn to this mill for grinding. His grandfather and great-grandfather had done it before him.

Knowing things like that always lent the mill a special interest to me. It was like a friend. More than once Joe and I had been fishing when a thunderstorm came up. That old mill was a cozy shelter. More than once Joe and I, on scorching summer nights, had slipped out and slept on the cool, stone floor. The year before, I was poking around in the upper loft and I found a handful of arrowheads someone had put on top of a beam, maybe a hundred years earlier, judging from the amount of dust covering them.

Joe and I had played among the ruins every summer since I could remember. The only uncomfortable thing about the mill was the constant danger that Kordick would show up and chase us. That happened a heap of times, but he never caught us.

Away up on the north side we had found a small window and by climbing the rafters we could stretch out on our tummies and see the top of our house and just about all of Joe's place and some distance beyond our town of Southfield.

That was some feeling—overlooking just about everybody who lived nearby. There were times when you could see the women hanging up clothes and the men working in the fields, and the cars rolling along the road. It was funny seeing them and not hearing them. It gave you a feeling of being bigger than you were and I liked that.

Well, it looked like that was gone now and I didn't cotton to the idea much. If I didn't like John Kordick before, I liked him less now. I figured he was stealing something that was mine, which wasn't reasonable, but I found a heap of items that even though your thinking and feeling isn't reasonable, you go right on thinking and feeling the way you want to. It wasn't that John Kordick didn't need a new house. He did. He lived in the sickest house in town and likely any change would have been for the best, even if he had moved into his barn. I'll say one thing, though, his carpenters knew what they were doing, so I stretched out, tying Rusty with my belt, and watched.

Along about four o'clock a brand new and elegant Cadillac pulled up the weedy lane and parked next to the carpenters' cars underneath an oak tree.

A man, oldish, but skinny and lively, climbed out of the car with a basset hound climbing out after him. The breeze stirred the stranger's hair considerably and he looked like a dandelion going to seed; not seedy, but sort of stately. Right off I noticed he was overly tall; maybe six-feet-five or there-abouts.

He walked around talking to the carpenters, pausing now and then to study their work. Once he pulled a roll of blueprints from his pocket and studied it with one of them. When they finished they called the other carpenters over and drove some stakes near where the cars were parked. I figured they were planning a garage.

At five o'clock the men gathered their tools, put them in

29

their cars and drove off, leaving the stranger and the hound standing under a crab apple tree.

I felt guilty, like I was snooping or a ''peeping tom'' as Mama would say, but I stayed anyway. The man must have walked around that house a dozen times, running his hands up and down the porch railing and fingering the stones. He stepped up on the porch and tested the new floor by jumping, not ungraceful, but sort of stiff-like.

He disappeared through the door, reappearing at each of the windows, testing the sash and studying the scenery.

At first he'd put his hand on the sill and study the earth below. Then he'd look at things near at hand, followed up with things far off, and finally he looked at the sky.

It took most of an hour before he completed the circuit of the house and reappeared on the porch again. I knew he was the one who was rebuilding the mill. John Kordick must have sold out. That's what he had meant that morning when he said things would be different if I were ever caught trespassing again.

My feelings went about as far as they could go, first in one direction and then another. As I watched that man move about I had the oddest sensation build up in me; a hunger, a wanting to be what I wasn't, or a wanting to have what I didn't, or go to places I hadn't been, or something. I'd had that feeling once before when a flock of geese went over one spring.

Next came an awful feeling of wanting to be the stranger and to be touching the sills and the railing and the stonework the way he did.

Anger came, because I knew I could never go in that old mill the way I used to.

The stranger sat on the porch steps with his back against one of the pillars. The basset, sad-eyed and deliberate, walked over and stretched out, with his head on the man's lap.

Believe it or not, from then on I had to fight liking this man, but I couldn't help myself. I liked him anyway. What I was seeing in the dusking evening was as pretty a picture as you'd likely see anywhere and the man was the center of it.

I knew that everything that was going on was important to him. He saw the blue heron feeding in the shallows of the pond. He saw the breeze licking the water's surface and he saw the white of the daisies with their yellow centers. He saw them the way I did, like they were things you'd like to write down and keep forever, just the way you were, and never once was he unmindful of the dog. His fingers worked around his ears and that dog was sharing something.

I couldn't stand it any longer. I backed off from my secret place.

I suppose it's nigh unto impossible to enjoy misery, but I was doing it anyway, walking through the silent woods along the bank of Canoe Brook with Rusty padding behind me.

Mama was waiting supper but she didn't scold though I was an hour and a half late. It was plain comfortable sitting there eating with no lights on, with the kitchen darkening as the day dimmed out of the sky. It was a relief not to have Lillie around.

I couldn't help myself; couldn't hold back from talking and I told Mama about the mill and the man and the dog.

Mama was quiet for a few minutes after I finished. "I know what you're going through." Her voice was that soft it almost stroked me. "I had a secret place when I was a girl. In proper weather I'd go there to read. During sad times it was the only place that could restore me."

Dusk was fading to darkness. Mama's face was heartlike in its paleness against her darker hair and the darkened kitchen. "I remember the day the caretaker discovered me and that was the end of that. What a tongue-lashing I received as he held me by the arm. He called me naughty and disrespectful, and me, as dumb as a fencepost not able to speak up and tell him I was none of those things, that I loved and cherished the place."

Mama was wistful. "That was the end of that," she repeated. "I went back there only once more. I went with Papa. I had told him about my affection for the place. Only Papa wasn't Papa then. It was a moonlight night. We walked up the lane between the row of trees to my secret place. We sat there for a little while and it was during our conversation Papa asked me to marry him. Some day I'd like to go back."

"Where was it, Mama?"

Mama laughed, and her face was almost gone in the paleness of the light. "It was the City of Heaven Cemetery. I can still remember the tombstone I used to rest my back against. It was a sickly cream-white stone with streaks of dark yellow in it. The inscription was barely legible but I worked it out:

TIMOTHY CALHOUN 1774-1836
BORN—LIVED—DIED
WORKED—LAUGHED—CRIED
DIDN'T DO AS WELL AS HE WANTED
BUT TRIED—TRIED—TRIED.

We laughed together.

Betsy broke the spell. "I got a secret. I got a secret!"

"What's your secret, Betsy?" I asked.

"I—I—I—" her mind was in the process of invention. "I love you. I love Mama. I love Lillie. I love Bob the Cat. I love Daisy."

"They're nice secrets," I said.

"I'm not done yet." Her tone was reproachful. "I love the chickens. I love the pigs, I love the swallows in the barn—and, and, and—"

Mama interrupted, "Aren't you forgetting someone?"

"Yup, Rusty."

"How about Papa?" Mama asked.

Betsy's voice took on her pouting tone, "Papa's not around to love much."

Mama was about to say something when Lillie called from outside. "Where is everybody? Anybody home? Turn the lights on quick! Open the door, I'm loaded down. Hurry!"

I didn't say it, but I sure wished she weren't home. Her barging in spoiled everything. I switched on the light and held the door open. She kicked off her shoes, dropped her bundles in a heap on the floor, dropped into a chair and took over the conversation.

I ducked out of the house as soon as I could. I did my evening chores in the dark, and not wanting to hear any more of Lillie I climbed the trellis and entered my bedroom through the window.

CHAPTER 3

THINGS DIDN'T JUMP OFF to a good start on Tuesday morning. Lillie was riding high with excitement at the breakfast table. How a body could get so worked up over a trip to Newark was more than I could figure. In my judgment her telling it was about as dry and boring as a thing could get and I couldn't understand Mama as she listened as bright and breathless as Lillie.

I should have gotten out of there but didn't. Lillie pounced on me. "Jerry, did you start borrowing lanterns?"

"No," I said, weak and sickly, hoping I'd fool her. "I feel poorly."

"Nonsense!" she snorted. "You get started today."

"Aw-w-w!"

"Jerry!"

"OK, Mama."

A thing like gathering lanterns for your sister's wedding doesn't sound too exciting, but it turned out pretty good. The womenfolk were worked up about the wedding and asked a heap of questions about the plans. I figured a dull thing like a wedding needed livening up so I spread it pretty thick in places about the decorations for the lawn and the people coming from all over. That worked pretty good, too. Those women went out of their way to find lanterns: in attics, basements, woodsheds and barns. By noon I had seventeen lined up on the back porch plus the promise of at least that many more.

Fact is, I did real good along another line, considering

how the women raided their iceboxes or pantries and came up with some interesting stuff. Before the morning was over I had slices of chocolate, vanilla and marble cakes, along with a square of gingerbread, two pieces of pie, apple and lemon. The lemon was faded some, to say the least. I figured Mrs. Canfield was about ready to feed it to the pigs, so I didn't mind hiding it inside my shirt and giving it to them personally after I left the house.

To top it off, I had two glasses of milk, a glass of lemonade, a glass of grape juice, and Mrs. Spears gave me a glass of something that was hard to figure. She claimed it was herb tea and tolerable good for growing boys, but it tasted more like how a fellow would expect a mud puddle to taste.

I wasn't too hungry at lunchtime, nor happy either when I reported to Lillie.

"You must have loafed on the job. Any fool could've gotten more lanterns than that. Why couldn't you get more?"

"Must be because I'm not a fool," I told her. Lillie didn't accept that as a reasonable answer.

I had a little time before I had to go to work and walked down to the mill. Things were lively. Stonemasons were beginning on the garage, carpenters were finishing up the windows and painters were concentrating on the porch.

I was home by two, changed my clothes and lit out for Beard's General Store.

Outsiders didn't think too much of our town of Southfield. Joe McCormick told me one time his dad heard a man say, "Blink your eyes when you're driving through Southfield and you'll clean miss it."

Another man was supposed to have piped up and said, "If you pass through it once you blink your eyes on purpose from then on to avoid seeing it."

A third man said, "Aw, you can tell it's there even when you blink—there's still the smell."

I think Joe's father stretched that conversation a bit, but unless you knew the town it wasn't much account.

Fat Lucy's place was on the southwest corner of the crossroads. That place was a bothering mystery to me and a

35

source of a lot more curiosity than I let on to anybody, including even Joe. It was an unpainted, shambly two-story building. The storefront window had what looked like a faded pink bedspread nailed over it. Even if the beadspread hadn't been there a body would have trouble looking inside because of the signs pasted all over the glass. I reckon some of those signs had been pasted up before I was born. Some had been up so long the sun had drained the printing clean off. The signs you could read advertised a lot of things: EAT BOND BREAD, SALADA TEA, COCA COLA, and others.

Another sign, painted on a board in blue and white, with real fancy letters said, LADIES INVITED. The bottom of the pink drape was considerably darker than the top and the sill turned out to be the cemetery for a considerable number of flies, moths and other insects.

Above the window in paint so faded you could barely see it, were the words, MARTHA WASHINGTON TEA ROOM, but in all the years I'd been around I'd never heard those words spoken once. It was always "Fat Lucy's place."

Three elm trees grew in front of Fat Lucy's place and circular benches had been built around the base of each. You could always count on those benches being well-crowded with men when the weather was tolerable. Talk was about the commonest thing there; gossip, stories about old times, and high-colored jokes.

Mama had caught me one time standing there and it was surprising to see how disturbed she was, and I got instructions never, "and I mean never, let me catch you anywhere near that place!"

From then on I was a little more careful, but I did manage to stop for a couple of minutes now and then.

Another building, a dead ringer for Lucy's except it had been kept up better, stood on the southeast corner. Clarence Gross' gas station and auto supply store occupied the bottom half. It was a pretty gaudy place with a circle of half-buried tires painted different colors. Inside the circle in front of the pumps Clarence had a sprightly mass of petunias.

A side door led up to the second floor of the building. This was the town's police station and lockup. Gus Lance was the only policeman and a good one; everybody said so. As near as I could see, he had one weakness, he was feather-headed about Miss Perry, the eighth-grade schoolteacher.

On the northeast corner was the town's only church. It wasn't any kind of a church, like Baptist, or Presbyterian, or Methodist. It was called Southfield's Church, and that was it.

Beard's General Store was on the northwest corner. The building had been owned by Arnie Beard's family since before the United States became the United States. Once it had been a stagecoach inn. George Washington was supposed to have slept there on more than one occasion, which was reasonable enough, for his headquarters were in Morristown only twenty miles away.

A body could see where Arnie's store had once been elegant, but someone had managed to spoil that, not that it was run down, but the front had been knocked out and replaced with display windows. A high porch, but narrow, ran across the front.

This porch was pretty handy. Sale items were stacked in heaps on either side of the door. Arnie was a swapper and a buyer and you could expect some pretty odd things to show up on that porch from time to time.

Two elms, as enormous as Fat Lucy's, grew in front of the store.

When I mounted the two steps to the porch I had to push around a wheelbarrow full of onions, a bucket of last year's bittersweet berries, an old rocking chair and heaps of other stuff to get to the door.

Arnie looked up from where he was working on his ledger behind the counter. "You're late again!" he roared. "Why can't you learn to get here on time?"

I looked at the clock hanging on the wall behind him. "I'm seven minutes early."

"Clock's slow!" Arnie snorted. "Get to work!"

That was like Arnie. Never once had I walked into that store without him telling me I was late.

37

"Stock's low. I want those shelves full."

I walked around the counter for my apron and saw that Arnie had his shoes off again. More and more lately he had been doing that. He didn't wear socks and he had his shoes laced and tied so loose they'd slip off easy. When a customer would come Arnie would glide his feet off the rung of the stool he sat on and into his shoes with no one the wiser. If I had feet like that I wouldn't want them in shoes either. They were pink and puffy with the toes crowding themselves so closely they fanned out away more than normal.

The first time I had seen this Arnie had reddened and looked away and then back helplessly. He didn't say anything, but I knew he was telling me not to tell anyone else and not to notice it myself from then on, and I didn't. I mean, I didn't tell anybody else, but I couldn't help looking because sometimes his feet would be almost normal but sickly pale and other times, well, like I said, they were a curiosity.

The rest of Arnie wasn't too normal either. He was pumpkin-headed and pumpkin-bodied. Winter and summer he wore a straw hat on his polished bald head, not that he was ashamed of his baldness, he wasn't, for no woman or girl ever entered the store without Arnie tipping his hat to her.

I hustled the stock and stacked the cans and jars on the shelves. "Arnie," I said, fishing for some information.

"Huh?"

"Do you know John Kordick's remodeling the mill by the pond?"

"No, he isn't. Now I'm not paying you for talking. I'm paying you for working."

I tore around for another five minutes figuring Arnie would say more and I was right.

"Kordick sold it to a man from New York. Wade's his name."

Mr. Kitzel, needing a haircut and shave as usual, pulled up in front of the store with a crate of chickens tied to the roof of his Model T. Arnie's feet slipped into his shoes like greased pigs.

Kitzel shuffled through the doorway looking hound-dog and shifty.

"Well, Kitzel, speak up, what can I do for you?"

"Mr. Beard," Kitzel drawled thinly, "you got any need for a crate of good layin' hens?"

"Nope. How much you asking?"

"Them hens is the cream of my crop." Mr. Kitzel picked up the tempo of his speech, which wasn't helpful for, being toothless as he was, he was hard to understand anyway, and all his words seemed to begin with *F*. "They're fine and fat. I was figurin' on gettin' fifty cents apiece for 'em."

Arnie glanced toward the hens. "Not interested. Sickly looking lot. Laying days is done. Fox wouldn't eat them. Hard to sell. Give you thirty cents apiece, throw in the crate."

"Aw-w-w," Kitzel's soiled right thumb jammed at his nose as though he were trying to shove it toward his left ear. "Aw-w-w, Mr. Beard, at that there price I'd lose money."

"I'd lose money if I paid any more for them."

"Cash, Mr. Beard?"

"Cash!" Arnie snorted, flipping his ledger open to the *K*'s. "It says here you owe me quite a piece."

"Aw-w-w-" Mr. Kitzel was agonizing. "I need cash, Mr. Beard. I need cash real bad."

"Half cash and half goes on your account, Kitzel."

Mr. Kitzel's thumb began to jab his nose upward. "Fine hens, fine hens," he moaned, shuffled his feet, looked at the ceiling, looked at the floor. "I could get three times that in Newark."

"Fine, fine," Arnie purred. "You go right ahead. Get them out from in front of the store. I can smell them in here already."

"All right, Mr. Beard," Kitzel moaned, "I'll take the three dollars and thank you for it. You put the other three on account."

Arnie took three dollars from the cash register and placed them on the counter. "Kitzel," he said, "try getting this bill worked down a little, will you?"

"Times is hard, Mr. Beard. Times is real hard. I can't never get ahead."

Arnie turned toward me. "Give him a hand unloading those hens, Jerry. Put them in the shade on the porch. Give them water and some stale bread. Tack up the FOR SALE sign."

Kitzel mumbled continually while we unloaded the hens. "A honest body can't never get ahead. Crooks like Beard never give us a break. I coulda gotten five times that price down in Newark."

I felt half mad at Arnie. "Why did you sell them, then, Mr. Kitzel?"

"I ain't got nothin' else to sell. I got a sick kid. These hens was eatin' more'n they was worth." He looked up sharply. "But they're fine hens, real fine. The only reason I sold them is 'cause I need money for medicine. Never would've done it if it wasn't for that. When a good father sees a kid sick he's willin' to make a sacrifice."

Mr. Kitzel let me unload the hens. When I entered the store Arnie snorted. "I hate to deal with that kind. Likely told you his family was starving, his kids needed new shoes, or his wife is sick."

It was surprising to see how close Arnie had come. I shot back, "You're wrong. One of his children is sick and needs medicine."

Arnie snorted again, "Sick child! Oh, no! Shiftless, worthless. If that kid is sick he'll stay sick. Could be those hens never saw Kitzel's place at all. I'd best check with Gus and see if some have been stolen lately."

Kitzel was still in front of the store cranking his car.

"He's going to buy medicine," I insisted.

Arnie said fiercely, "The only medicine Kitzel's interested in is the kind he can get in Fat Lucy's back room."

Kitzel's car backfired and roared. He didn't bother to turn it around. He backed it across the street, parked it in the shade of one of the elms, leaped out and almost ran into Fat Lucy's place.

It bothered me some to see what a fool I'd made of myself and I thought Arnie would say so, but he didn't.

"You, Jerry! I'm not paying you to look out the window at trash like that. Get to work!"

Joe Ledden came into the store. "Are those poorly, run-down chickens for sale, Arnie?"

"That's what the sign says," Arnie answered, soft as cotton. "Price is ten dollars plus two for the crate. Twelve all together." He slipped his straw hat off his head, and holding it between his thumb and forefinger explored his baldness with his free fingers. He always did that when he was dickering and as usual, the third finger followed the purple line of a vein that ran oddly from above his left eye to the back of his right ear.

"I'll take the whole lot off your hands for nine dollars."

"I thought I said ten, plus two," Arnie said with a surprised tone to his voice. He turned to me. "Isn't that what I said, Jerry, ten plus two? I didn't say nine, did I? Them is laying hens, fine and fat, and I did say ten dollars plus two."

"Nine and a quarter."

"Eleven seventy-five for the works."

It took twenty minutes to make that sale but it was made at ten fifty, and both men were pleased with themselves when it was over.

The rest of my day was dullish. At twenty-five after six I took off my apron and hung it up on a hook beside the meat cleaver.

Arnie exploded, "What are you doing?"

"Going home. Six is quitting time."

"'Tain't six yet. Clock's fast."

I never did see anybody so anxious to get the last lick of work out of a body. I never did know anyone who could lecture on success like he did either.

"Afraid of work, are you? Clock watcher. You'll never get ahead. Soft, that's what this generation is. When I was your age I was working fifteen hours a day, six days a week right here in this store."

"For ten cents an hour?" I asked. Right off I knew I'd made a mistake.

"Ten cents!" Arnie snorted. "I got five cents an hour."

Arnie was still talking when I closed the door gently behind me.

The town was quiet except for the voices drifting from the darkened doorway of Lucy's place. Kitzel's truck was still there and I heard his mousy laughter as I walked by.

Mama was some disturbed when I entered the kitchen. "Every night it's the same thing, Jerry; late for supper."

"Blame Arnie. I'd never come home if he had his way."

Lillie was furious. "It seems to me, Jerry, you'd speak up for yourself. Speak up for your own rights. You'll never get anywhere letting people tramp over you the way you do. Besides, I wanted you home at six. Mrs. Sebastian called and she has four lanterns. I want you to hustle over and get them."

I looked at Lillie. I started to talk soft. "You're right, Lillie. I ought to start standing up for my rights and I'm going to start right now." My voice rose a pitch. "If you want those lanterns, Lillie," my voice went up to its top pitch, "go get them yourself!"

Lillie snatched the flyswatter from its hook behind the stove and headed for me. I stood my ground.

Mama said sharply, "That's enough, both of you! Lillie, Jerry gathered lanterns all morning and outside of a little while after lunch he hasn't had a minute to himself. He still has to milk the cow and feed the chickens and pigs. I suggest you let him alone."

That sent Lillie into a pout, and it turned out to be a nice quiet meal, after all.

Later, when I was doing my chores, Joe McCormick came over. "Hey, Joe, what got into you yesterday?"

Joe growled, "That George Hostler. If I don't get even with him I'm going to know the reason why."

"That guy!" I heaved the hay fork at a bale clear at the other end of the barn and got special delight out of it when it smacked the hay dead center with its handle quivering. "What did he do this time?"

"It's not what he did, it's what he claimed I did. Last

Sunday he wanted the day off so he came around begging, 'I'll tell you what I'll do, Joey boy. I'll do all your chores tomorrow, if you'll do mine today. I'll give you fifty cents besides.' I shoulda known better but I gave in. Well, yesterday morning after he fed the hogs he forgot to close the pen. Hogs got out, dumped a can of milk, busted a bag of chicken feed, rooted around Mom's tulips, plus a variety of other things. When Pop saw it he wasn't too happy. He crawled all over me. I was explaining how it wasn't my fault, when who walks up but good ol' George. How a man could stand there and lie like he did was more than I could see. Instead of him looking like the liar he made me look like one. He said there was no truth to me doing his chores on Sunday, that he hadn't done my chores, nor even been near the pigpen on Monday.

"Pop was pretty riled. He took it out on me, not only for leaving the pigpen open, but because he figured I was lying. I'm not supposed to budge off the farm once this week." He laughed. "Pop and Mom are out visiting my aunt tonight, and old George is off to Lucy's place, so here I am."

We drifted down to Kordick's pond. "Wait 'til you get a slant of that old mill, are you in for a surprise!"

The change didn't rest too good with Joe. He whispered from our hiding place in the brush, "Everything a fellow likes real good gets taken away. Last month Pop snatched my BB gun because I put the skimpiest little hole in the barn window. After I'd babied Meadow Blossom from a calf and nursed her into the likeliest looking heifer on the place Pop took her to auction."

"I know," I said. I thought of Papa coming into the barn with his suitcases and then going off on another business trip, but I didn't say anything about it.

On the way back to my house we took to talking about George. "I've got to square with him," Joe growled.

"I have an idea!" I said. "George is always braggin' about how he doesn't need any alarm clock to wake him up in the morning. He's always braggin' how his eyes are that sensitive that the first glow of morning light rouses him. Now suppose no first glow of light reached his eyes. I mean, what if we covered over his window with cardboard tonight when he's sound asleep?''

Joe caught the idea with glee. ''Why, good old George would oversleep. Good ol' George wouldn't get up to milk the cows. Pop's touchy about those cows and he'd get plenty stirred up. Good ol' George would get blamed and I'd be about as happy as a fellow could get.''

''You think it might work?''

''Jerry, he doesn't have an alarm clock. He doesn't have a shade in the window. He's always up at dawn every morning. Yessiree! I think it would work!''

We made arrangements to meet later and I went to bed about as happy as could be.

About twelve o'clock I skinned into my clothes, went out the window, climbed down the roof and trellis and within a jiffy we were walking toward Joe's house.

George lived in the hired man's shanty; a small, one-room building located behind the barn. We had no trouble at all covering the window with cardboard and within an hour I was back in bed.

Joe was at my house at eleven thirty the next morning about as gay as a fellow could be.

''How did it go?'' I asked.

''Perfect, perfect, perfect!'' Joe bubbled. ''Along about four o'clock I heard Pop get up and I remembered that he was going to take a load of hogs down to the market. I thought at first this would spoil our plans but it didn't.

''I didn't bother to go back to sleep. Things were quiet until about eight o'clock when the cows started to fuss a bit. Ma was in the basement washing clothes so she didn't notice which was a break for us, for if she had gone to George's place to wake him up she would've seen the cardboard and *pow!* That would've been that! Well, anyway, I can tell you those cows made a fearful racket by the time nine-thirty came. I kept out of sight and when I heard Pop's truck come in the driveway I sneaked over, slipped the cardboard from George's window and scooted around to the barn and hid in the loft.

"Those cows were sure raising a fuss; hungry as they were and needing milking as bad as they did. Pop came into the barn and stared sort of stunned-like when who comes in but George, rubbing his eyes and yawning. Pop blew sky-high and bawled George out something fierce. George kept mumbling over and over again, 'Can't understand it. Never overslept before.' Pop kept on ragging at him and George got mad and shouted at Pop.

"Well, that did it. Pop told him he was fired, told him to get off the place and never come back again. George went into high gear, and I'll tell you, the air was blue."

"What would happen if George ever found out what we did?" I asked.

Joe frowned. "I'll tell you, Jerry, I try not to think of that because George was a wild man when he left. If he found out we had anything to do with it—wowee!" Joe shrugged his shoulders and ran a finger significantly across his throat. "Now I'm going to have to get home because Pop's pretty touchy about things. I'll have extra work to do until we get another hired man." A grin returned to his face. "I'll tell you one thing, though. It's worth it."

I was as happy as Joe. I figured it was as good a way as any to get back at George. I kept on thinking so until after I went to the store to work. In the middle of the afternoon Mrs. McCormick came in.

Arnie tipped his straw hat and rubbed his hand over his sweaty bald head. "Heard you had quite a fight out at your place this morning?"

Mrs. McCormick looked surprised. "How did you find out? I'm sure Si didn't say anything."

"George Hostler was in here around noontime," Arnie explained. "From what he said your husband was pretty unreasonable firing him the way he did."

It was plain Mrs. McCormick was upset. "I'm glad that man's gone. I never did like him: braggy, loud, evil-eyed, never could face a body when he talked. He was always accusing Joe of one thing or another and you could never believe a word he said."

"Well," Arnie said, "from what he said you haven't seen the last of him."

"What?"

Arnie leaned over the counter in a confidential sort of way. "I'll tell you, Mrs. McCormick, I'd keep my eye peeled if I were you. He claims he's going to get revenge if it's the last thing he does. Says you people are going to pay, the way you've mistreated him."

That shook Mrs. McCormick. "He's the kind of man who'd do it, too. I know that," she whispered hoarsely.

It shook me, too, and I figured maybe Joe and I had gone too far.

Arnie filled Mrs. McCormick's order and she left in a hurry. Arnie had slipped off his shoes again and almost at once put them on. Another customer was coming.

The stranger from Kordick's pond walked through the door, leathery looking, big-nosed, large-mouthed, hollow-cheeked, craggy-chinned and altogether the homeliest but pleasantest looking man you'd ever want to see and about the smilingest man I ever saw, too.

He moved slowly toward the counter, glancing around the shelves as he came. His eyes looked into mine for a flashing moment. He winked. I was that surprised I didn't wink back but I wanted to.

Arnie said in his best new-customer tone as he reached over the counter with his hand, "Welcome to Southfield, sir. You must be the gentleman who purchased Kordick's place."

"News travels."

"A town this size has very few secrets. You are the newcomer, aren't you?"

"I'm Julius Wade, and true enough, I've purchased that land." The two shook hands and it was startling to see the long, brown, bony fingers cradle Arnie's whitish, thick, stubby ones.

Mr. Wade said, "I have a crew of carpenters and masons who voted to have a dinner at my expense: steak, mind you, baked potatoes and ice cream."

"Steak we have, the best, tender and juicy." Arnie headed for the cooler.

The order was a whopper and as Arnie filled it he asked questions in what he thought was an offhand, disinterested way, but he couldn't hide his curiosity. "Planning to spend the summers here?"

Mr. Wade laughed, and I figured he was laughing at Arnie's curiosity. "I'll be here year 'round."

"John Kordick set a high price on that land."

"We bargained some and came to an agreement."

"You're from New York?"

"Yes. I taught at Columbia University for the last thirty years."

I packed the order in a box while Arnie added the list of figures he'd jotted down on a paper bag. "Twenty-two dollars and fifty nine cents," Arnie announced.

Mr. Wade took bills from his wallet, added a pamphlet from his coat pocket and handed them to Arnie. "Mr. Beard, man can't live by bread alone, and I'd like to share with you some spiritual food. Read this pamphlet and the next time I drop by perhaps we could discuss it."

Arnie glanced at the title of the pamphlet and the expression on his face changed. Before he had been friendly natural-like, now he was being friendly in an unnatural way. "I'll glance at it if I have time," he said as he laid the pamphlet on the cash register and proceeded to give Mr. Wade his change.

The newcomer left. Arnie perched on top of his stool again and slipped off his shoes. A patch of sun touched his feet; they were bright pink, and his toes were puffed and fitted snuggly together looking like five rolls baking in a pan.

He picked up the pamphlet while I pulled dead leaves from the cabbage and lettuce. He read for quite a while and snorted disgustedly when he finished. "Well, it looks like we have another crackpot in town."

"He seemed like a nice man," I countered.

Arnie held the pamphlet in his left hand and clicked his right finger against it impatiently. He read the title,

47

"WHERE WILL YOU SPEND ETERNITY: IN HEAVEN OR IN HELL?" He opened the page and read: " 'Every person upon the earth was conceived in iniquity and born in sin.' " He fumed. "Illogical nonsense! This is an insult to parenthood." He paused; studied the pamphlet. "Listen to this, 'Since man is a sinner he is in danger of God's judgment for the sin he has committed. Every sinner stands doomed before God unless he accepts God's gift to the world, Jesus Christ, as his Saviour. When the sinner accepts Christ the penalty for sins is removed and God forgives him.' "

Arnie sucked in his breath, slapped the paper, exploded, "Bosh!" and read on, his voice high and angry. " 'The person who rejects Christ as Savior will be punished in hell.' "

I'd never seen Arnie so upset. I didn't understand everything that he read, but I figured on having a little fun. "That seems reasonable to me," I said in my soberest tone.

"Reasonable!" Arnie's face was a light purple. "Reasonable! What would a kid like you know about it?"

"Well, my Sunday school teacher says things like that. And it seems a lot like Pastor Wallace's preaching sometimes."

"Wallace! That addlepated nincompoop! What does he do every Sunday? Stands up in front of the same little flock of people, leads them in singing the same little songs. Ha!" he shouted. "I've heard them when I've been working here in the store Sunday mornings. I've heard them singing, 'I come to the garden alone, while the dew is still on the roses. And the voice I hear, falling on my ear, the Son of God discloses. He walks with me and He talks with me, and He tells me I am His own. . . .' Ha, you see, I haven't been in church for forty years and I know the words by heart just listening. I know those people. None of them ever go to the garden to talk to the Son of God alone. They go to pull weeds. They go to pick flowers. They go to get vegetables and other things, too. The only things they hear is the buzz of mosquitoes, flies or bees," he said darkly. "And there's another one that gives me a laugh, too. 'I'll go where you want me to go, Dear Lord.

48

I'll do what you want me to do.' Where do they go? And what do they do after they get done singing? Home, that's where. Home to eat a whopping big Sunday dinner, and then they go to bed for the afternoon. Ha, I'll tell you, there's nothing to it.

"The church is supposed to be a lighthouse in town, supposed to be the headquarters for the salvation of every man. Ha!" Arnie was going full blast now. "That church has all it can do to save itself. Every week what happens? There's a bake sale or a bazaar or a rummage sale. I can count on somebody coming here once a month and asking for something to sell at one of their doings. 'Mr. Beard,' they say, 'would you care to donate something for the support of the church?' I'm laughing to myself when I say, 'Sure, Mrs. Ebberding, how would a quart of dill pickles do?' 'Wonderful!' Mrs. Ebberding says right back. 'Every little bit helps, and we must keep the lighthouse open, you know.' It looks to me like I'm saving the church."

I'd finished the vegetable bin. Arnie glared at me. "I'm not paying you to stand there! Clean that candy case!"

I couldn't help adding, "Well, Mr. Wade looks like an intelligent man. If he taught at the university he'd be smart enough to see if a thing were true or not."

"Keep still!" Arnie shouted, "or I'll be getting another boy." He crumpled up the pamphlet and threw it on the floor and for the rest of the afternoon he was as touchy as a bull, being nice and sweet only when customers came in.

It was about quarter to six when Mr. Wade returned. "Forgot all about salt," he told Arnie. "I'll take a box, and a pound of butter, too."

"Mr. Wade," Arnie emphasized the name heavily. "You've invaded the privacy of my mind." He picked up the crumpled pamphlet. "It's your privilege to believe this if you want to, but don't come shoving that stuff down my throat."

Mr. Wade smiled, unconcerned and easylike. "I'm glad you read it, Mr. Beard. Now, if I could have the salt and butter."

"Jerry, a box of salt and a pound of butter, quick!"

Arnie ordered, then faced Mr. Wade and slapped his hand down on the pamphlet he had laid out on the counter. "You expect me to believe that?"

"You could if you wanted to," Mr. Wade said casually.

"I don't want to."

I put the salt and butter on the counter.

"I don't want to," Arnie repeated and in the same voice said, "That'll be thirty-seven cents."

Mr. Wade dug the change from his pocket, pulled another pamphlet from his coat and handed it to Arnie. "Mr. Beard," he said gently, "I'd like you to read this one, but if you don't want to, throw it away."

Mr. Wade left the store and climbed into his car. Arnie stared after him vacantly. Slowly he turned and looked at the pamphlet reading grimly aloud, " 'Four Things God Wants You To Know.' "

He looked out at Mr. Wade who by this time was pulling away. "There's a fifth thing God wants me to know: avoid crackpots." He turned on me. "What are you staring at? Sweep out the store!"

"I'm going home. It's twenty after six."

"You know that clock's fast."

I hung up my apron and started for the door, leaving Arnie hunched over the counter reading the pamphlet.

CHAPTER 4

PAPA CAME HOME on Saturday and we had a high-style meal at noontime as we always did when Papa returned from a trip.

The following Monday Papa took Mama, Lillie and Betsy down to East Orange to see an old maid aunt who was an invalid and who would not be able to get to the wedding. I didn't want to go, for it got pretty dull sitting in a stuffy little apartment listening to a lot of talk about people I didn't know. Lillie was anxious. Aunt Helen was loaded with money and I figured Lillie figured she would get a juicy big gift.

Before they left Mama said, "Here's a list of things I want from Arnie. Sometime during the day pick them up."

After they left I finished up my chores and decided to get the shopping done so I would have time for a little fishing.

On the way to the store I passed John Kordick's farm. Papa always said Kordick's house had probably been built by the same man that built ours. True enough, they were shaped alike, but the resemblance stopped there. His was the most run-down place in town. The clapboard siding was split, curled and weather-whomped to a blackish brown. The top bricks on both chimneys had tumbled down leaving jagged, uneven edges. The front porch sagged toward the middle. The rackety steps had been repaired a number of times by nailing old boards on top.

At first glance you would wonder if anyone lived there but a second glance showed someone did, for uncurtained windows were spotlessly clean. That was the work of John

Kordick's wife, Mousy Millie, as everyone called her.

She was a wispy woman and always dressed in sober clothes, gray usually, and way out of style. At best guess she weighed maybe ninety pounds: haggard face, wrinkly-browed, big-eyed—blackish and starry—hair pulled back in a bun, whispery-shy voiced when she spoke, which was seldom.

Everybody felt sorry for Millie, and everybody wanted to help her but no one did: no one dared and probably no one knew how.

There had been three boys born into the family; big, strapping fellows who were forced to drop out of school when they were big enough to do work on the farm. I remembered seeing them but didn't know them, being way too young for them to pay attention to me. From what I heard Papa, Arnie and other people say, they were about as nice boys as you could find anywhere, but living under John Kordick's roof was too much for them and each one left home as soon as he was old enough to shift for himself.

By the looks of the house, the barn and the farm, and by the looks of John and Millie, you would think they were the poorest people in town, but that wasn't so. From what I heard Papa say, John Kordick's father and grandfather before him had been wonderfully successful farmers and all the property and money had fallen into John's hands at their death, but he was so miserly and stingy he'd never spend a cent unless he had to. And he kept right on making money, too, selling some of the land now and then, farming a little, buying horses and cows, or anything else, for that matter, real cheap and selling it high.

Well, anyway, I was just about past Kordick's place when I heard a lively tap on the window. I turned and saw John beckoning to me. John never called me except to warn me about trespassing. I figured that was what he was up to now. I decided to run rather than get bawled out, when John opened the door.

"Jerry, Jerry, you come here. I wanna do a favor for you."

That surprised me so I hesitated, then walked slowly through the weedy lawn toward the porch.

John emerged, all 390 pounds of him, barefoot, moist-lipped, a large wooden match hanging from the corner of his mouth. Rolls of fat bulged from under his chin. Wet sweat patches circled under his armpits making the gray shirt black-ish. Lines of sweat moistened a strip about two inches either side of his suspender straps.

He stared down at me over his pouch. The matchstick rolled from one side of his mouth to the other and twice he ran his finger along his lower lip to remove the beads of moisture accumulating there.

"Wanna make some money?" His jowls sort of flat-tened out as he spoke.

"How?" I asked.

"My sour cherries are overripe. I'm feeling too poorly to pick 'em myself. A day's work'd do it."

Mousy Millie came out and stood behind her husband. She seemed about to say something, thought better of it, wagged her head slightly and retreated into the house without him knowing she had made an appearance.

It had me guessing for a minute, but John Kordick was talking, "I seen your folks go by."

"They went down to see my aunt."

"Won't be home 'til late?"

"No—" I said slowly. "Mama said not to expect them 'til maybe ten o'clock tonight."

"Well now, if you could show them a five-dollar bill when they came home wouldn't that please them some?"

"You mean you'll give me five dollars for a day's work picking cherries?"

The matchstick rolled to the left and back to the right corner of his mouth. "I'm a fool for givin' so much, but I want them picked, so, yup, five dollars'll be the price."

I had never made five dollars in a week. While none of the fellows ever wanted to work for John Kordick because of his nasty ways, the offer was too tempting to turn down. "Yes, sir, I'll do it."

I followed Kordick around the house to the barn where we threw boxes on his truck. When we had enough he drove me to the cherry orchard a quarter of a mile behind the house.

"I'll leave the truck here," he said. "When you fill the boxes load them on and make sure the sun don't get at 'em."

It was pleasant enough picking the cherries and while they were the sour variety their ripeness gave them a tangy sweetness that made them tasty. It was a wild sort of a place and I had a lot of birds for company, and by the looks of some of the cherries, the birds liked them as much as I did.

At noon I went home for a sandwich and a glass of milk and was back before Kordick knew I was gone. I guess it was four-thirty when he put in an appearance. He walked around slowly checking the trees I had finished.

"There's a limb you missed," he growled.

I glanced at the limb and I don't believe there were more than seven cherries on the tip end that I had missed, but the fuss he made about it made me wonder if he was going to cut the price he had offered.

He walked under me and stood below the last tree still to be picked. "It seems to me you could've been done before this."

"I've kept at it," I countered. "There must be between four and five hundred pounds on the truck." Right then I remembered that other farmers were paying two cents a pound. I felt cheated.

"Anyone know you're working for me?" he asked casually.

"No, sir, I haven't seen a soul all day."

Kordick stood in the shade watching me. I finished the tree I was working on and moved the ladder to the last one. He helped and insisted on leaning it against a skimpy limb.

"I don't think that limb'll hold me."

"It's strong enough," he growled.

"It might break."

"It's an old tree, needs trimming anyway."

The limb wasn't much bigger around than my thumb, but it was his tree, so I started to climb. I hadn't gone up three rungs when the limb snapped. The ladder tipped forward and came to rest on a sturdy limb.

I glanced at Kordick but he wasn't looking, he was walking toward the house.

About twenty minutes later he returned, climbed into the truck without a word and drove off, carting the cherries away. I finished the top of the tree and set the cherries I had picked nearby and was working on the low limbs when I heard a startling sound. I swung about and saw Kordick huffing toward me.

"You gave me a start, Mr. Kordick, I'm—" I started to tell him I was almost finished but I never got the words out. He lumbered on as though to thump me into the ground, shirt dripping wet with perspiration and pants the same. His thin-nish red-gray hair hung plastered to his forehead and cheeks. His face glistened with perspiration. His little eyes bulged.

I started to back away but I didn't make it. A heavy, meaty hand reached out and his thumb and forefinger clamped down on my left ear with such viciousness I yowled.

"Dirty, thievin' kid!" he roared, sucking in his breath between every word. "Caught you, didn't I? Knew someone was stealin' my cherries. Caught you red handed, didn't I? Sure glad I had the rest of them picked."

"I—I—" I started to talk but the fingers crimped to-gether and another yowl left my lips.

He dragged me back about ten feet and looked up at the tree. "Look at that! You broke a limb, you dirty crook!"

"I—"

Kordick's fingernails dug into my ear and I felt blood. He pulled downward and I went to my knees. I caught a glimpse of Mousy Millie standing a few feet away. She looked something like a gray fencepost; hands at her sides, with an expression of heartache on her face. "Mr. Kor—"

"Shut up!" he boomed. He yanked me to my feet and loomed over me with his face not more than four inches from mine. The odor from his perspiring body hit my nostrils. "I want you off my place in one minute. If I ever catch you around here again I'll whump your pants off. I'll be seein' your old man and I'll be tellin' him about your thievin' ways, you miserable, thievin' pup!'' He sent me sprawling and I came up off the ground fighting mad.

"You!'' I shouted. "You're the thief! You're the cheat! You promised me five dollars! You—''

I got no further. He lunged for me and sent a kick my way. I stepped lively, dodged it, tripped, sprawled, saw Kordick coming for me again, rolled out of reach, scrambled to my feet and stood defiantly. I'd been mad a lot of times in my lifetime but never like that. I could feel blood trickling down my cheek from my ear. My head felt as though it had been plunged into boiling water. I turned to Mousy Millie. Her hands were drawn up and clasped under her chin. Her thin lips seemed to have disappeared—her mouth seemed nothing more than a little cut in her face. Her eyes were closed.

Kordick caught up a stub of wood and was bearing down on me, jowls purply red, eyes bulging. "Get!''

There was nothing I could do so I turned my back and walked toward home.

I admit it, I cried. I cried on the way home and the tears didn't stop when I looked at my bloodied ear in the bathroom mirror, nor did they stop when I went down to the brook for a swim. When no more tears would come I still felt as though I were crying inside and each time I thought of Kordick a new fury built up. I guess I must have said the words over a hundred times, "I'll get even with you, see if I don't, Kordick. Just see if I don't!'' I meant it, too. I meant it as much as I'd ever meant anything in my life.

My ear began to swell up and the side of my face burned uncomfortably. There were three gashes where Kordick's fingernails had cut me, and a longer gash where Kordick had actually pulled apart my skin between my ear and the side of my head. It was a hot, sweaty night and when the salty perspiration touched my wounds it added to my misery and my anger.

I ate a little and waited up for my folks to tell them what had happened, but by the time nine-thirty came I was so sleepy

I went to bed. I dropped off to sleep trying to think of some way to even the score with Kordick. How long I slept I don't know, but I was awakened by the distant sound of voices. I heard Lillie coming upstairs with Betsy and wondered why Papa and Mama didn't follow.

Twenty minutes passed. The back door opened and closed. Papa's voice came up the stairs, "Jerry, come to the kitchen."

I pulled on my overalls. When I reached the kitchen Mama was at the stove making coffee. Papa was at the table, sober-faced and stern.

Mama turned and sucked in her breath when she saw my ear. Papa studied me for a minute and frowned. "What happened, Jerry?" he asked.

I didn't want the tears to come but they sprang to my eyes. Papa looked away. I tried to talk. I couldn't. All I could do was sob.

"Jerry, when we pulled into the driveway John Kordick was waiting there. He did a lot of talking. He said a lot of things. Tell us your side of the story."

I still couldn't talk. My throat seemed to be choked off.

Papa went on. "He said he caught you stealing cherries, claimed you broke a large limb on his best tree, claimed you used some pretty coarse language when he caught you. Claimed you picked up a stick and tried to hit him."

The more Papa said the angrier I became. Finally I found my voice. I screamed, "That John Kordick's a liar—a dirty liar!"

Mama gasped, "Jerry!"

"I don't care!" the words flowed now. "He's a liar! This morning I was on my way up to Arnie's with the list you gave me." Only then did I remember that I'd forgotten to do Mama's shopping, but I didn't bother to mention it. "He promised me five dollars for picking cherries. I worked hard and I didn't break the limb. That was his fault." I told everything, not leaving out a single thing. When I finished I sat down at the table and laid my head on my hands. Sobs shook me so I hurt across my chest, and my head, already hot, grew hotter and my ear throbbed and ached.

Papa spoke and his voice was trembly. "I believe you, Jerry. I believe you." He shook his head from side to side and said, "John Kordick wanted fifty dollars for the damage you had done."

"You didn't pay it?"

"Of course not. I told Kordick I wanted to hear your side of the story."

"Good," I said. "And he owes me five dollars, and even if I get it he'll still be cheating me because picking those cherries was worth more than that."

Papa shook his head. "I'm going to see John about that, but I'm afraid it won't do any good. He's cagey. You see, Jerry, he's threatening to have you arrested for trespassing and vandalism, but don't you worry about that, he's bluffing and I won't pay him."

"Gus would never believe him."

Papa gave a laugh, sort of sick without humor. "Gus wouldn't believe him. You can be sure of that. Gus has reason not to believe John, but John has a way of making things uncomfortable, to say the least."

"You'd better tell Jerry everything," Mama said.

"I suppose I had better," Papa sighed. "Kordick never gives up on a thing, Jerry. I've known him all my life. He bullyrags at a thing. Keeps after it and keeps after it, and makes life generally uncomfortable. He had me over a barrel once. I was young and wanted to go into the clothing business up where Joe Vendetta has his shoe shop now." (Joe Vendetta had a one-room building two hundred yards beyond the church.)

"John heard about it and offered to lend me the money. I borrowed two thousand dollars. Well, the business failed. It took me some time to get the two thousand paid, plus the interest. When I figured it was done John claimed another thousand, took me to court. In my ignorance I had signed a paper. I thought it was the same one I had read at my previous meeting with him. It wasn't. I had signed a paper saying I had borrowed three thousand."

Papa laughed again, sort of sickly and without humor. "That taught me something, Jerry. And this whole mess ought to teach you something."

It didn't make sense to me. "Couldn't we go to court and make him pay? What about my ear?"

"Oh, he has that covered. He claims he boxed your ear when you came at him with the club."

Mama said, "Jerry, you stay away from John Kordick."

"Don't worry, I intend to!"

Mama went on, "When that man's in a rage there's no telling what he'll do." Mama paused and said, "Poor Millie! How often I've seen her bruised face. She never said, but I knew John did it."

After a while we relaxed. Mama bathed my ear in a solution that helped cool it some. Papa suggested another cup of coffee and we talked. We kept talking until after three o'clock in the morning.

When I went to bed I felt comfortable in one way, but more determined than ever to fix Kordick.

CHAPTER 5

I DIDN'T WAKE UP the following morning until nine o'clock. Papa had already left on a business trip to Trenton but I found he had done all my chores.

Mama smiled when I came back into the kitchen. "Papa figured you'd want to sleep in this morning so he got up a little early to help you out."

"He sure didn't get much sleep, did he?" Suddenly I felt as though a ball of barbed wire was jammed down in my chest. The experiences of the day before flooded back. "Poor Papa," I said. "Kordick cheats him, Kordick plagues him. He gets no sleep. He does my chores. Poor Papa!"

"Papa wouldn't want you to feel sorry for him, Jerry."

"I know," I said and then I said something I shouldn't have said. "I'll fix him, that Kordick. You just wait and see. I'll fix him!"

Mama was startled. "Jerry, don't you dare do a thing! You promise? You promise me?"

I crossed my fingers and said, "I promise, but that Kordick's mean. I mean, really mean, and snaky sneaky. I should've been smarter than to work for him in the first place. Nobody in town ever works for him, and he's never kept a hired man more than a week."

Betsy came into the kitchen singing, "Jerry's bad, Jerry's bad, Jerry's bad again!"

Before I had a chance to put her straight Lillie came in with her hair knotted up in paper curlers, yawning, with sleep still in her eyes. She looked at my ear, puffed, scratched and red and said, "It serves you right for stealing cherries. The way you're going you'll end up in the state prison before you're eighteen."

"Lillie!" Mama said with surprising sharpness, and with a tone seldom heard or used except when she was very, very angry. "You're getting married in a few weeks. This means you're supposed to be an adult. Act like one."

"He stole Kordick's cherries, didn't he?" Lillie snapped defiantly.

"He did not," Mama said flatly. She went on to explain what had happened. Do you think that Lillie would change her nasty ways? She would not. She said if she had to choose between the two stories she'd pick Kordick's.

I got up from the table saying, "It's too bad Roger can't see what a sweet-looking and sweet-sounding girl you are now. He'd likely marry anybody else but you."

I bolted out the screen door and went to the barn, dismissing Lillie from my mind. I didn't dismiss Kordick from my mind, though. The more I thought about it the more I determined to get even with him. I thought of a bunch of ideas: to let the air out of his truck tires, open up his chicken coop and let the chickens out, turn his pigs loose, break his windows, but none of the ideas were any good.

A little after two o'clock I headed for the store. As I approached Kordick's place I ducked into the woods on the other side of the house and kept out of sight. When I was across from his house I looked through the brush and saw fat John sitting on the porch in a rocking chair sound asleep, mouth open, bare feet on the railing, hands folded on his pouch. I found a stone about half the size of my fist and heaved it against the house above the porch over his head. That stone made considerable racket as it hit the roof and rolled off into the weeds.

The rocking chair went back, bare feet slapped the floor. Kordick rose up, half conscious and staggering and bellowing, "Millie!" Louder, "Millie!" Still louder, "MILLIE!"

The front door opened and Mousy Millie came through the doorway. Kordick proceeded to give her a bawling out for waking him up and told her if she did it again he'd kick her off the place.

Mousy Millie didn't say a word. She reentered the house and closed the door, while John climbed into the rocking chair, shifted himself around a half dozen times until he was comfortable, put his feet on the railing, folded his hands, opened his mouth and went to sleep again.

I went on to the store, sorry I'd been the cause of Millie's getting a bawling out, and more determined than ever to get revenge.

It wasn't until four o'clock that afternoon that a plan burst upon my mind. I was delivering an order to Mrs. Ebberding. On the way I noticed a raggety-clothed scarecrow in the garden patch beside the home of Jack Spear. I knew instantly what I was going to do and I got to thinking about it so lively for the rest of the afternoon that Arnie lost his temper at least seven times, accusing me of loafing, laziness and all manner of other things, but my thoughts were so satisfying I didn't mind.

That night after Mama and Lillie went to bed I dressed, went out the window, down the trellis and into the darkness. I thought of getting Joe McCormick to help me, but decided against this. I figured when you're doing something questionable it's best to do it alone because if two people know it there's double the chance of getting it talked about.

I slipped past his house, past Kordick's, keeping well hidden in case cars came. I went behind Arnie's store to the center of town and walked in the brush along Southfield Road, to Spear's place.

It wasn't much of a job hauling the scarecrow home. I hid it in the hayloft, figuring on going to work on my plan the next morning.

Lillie spoiled my plans, for she insisted on sending me around to gather lanterns. Papa, Mama and Lillie had borrowed quite a few besides the ones I had already gathered and there were about fifty on the barn floor when I started, and by one o'clock I had nine more, for Arnie donated the ones he had used on his delivery wagon before he got a car.

You'd be surprised how many different kinds of lanterns there were, but they all had two things in common: smoky chimneys and oil-stained bases.

Thursday wasn't much better, for Lillie set me to cleaning the chimneys and what a job that was! Some of that oily smoke along with accumulations of dust had been on those lanterns for thirty years.

Mama and Lillie, along with Betsy, caught the early bus to Newark for a shopping spree on Friday. That gave me a chance to go to work on the scarecrow. I soaked newspaper in water and added flour until it was a pasty mass. From this I shaped the head, ears, nose, eyes and mouth. I did my best to make the face look like John Kordick, and while the finished job was crude, there was a resemblance.

I stuffed more hay in the coat and trousers until the stomach was as big as I could get it. I found a pair of old boots and used them instead of the original straw feet the scarecrow had. I made a gun; a broom handle for the barrel and a piece of two-by-four for the stock.

The hardest job I had was to get Mr. Strawman's arms to look natural as they aimed the gun at a distant target. Hands were made from the paper, flour and water mixture. By the time I was finished, Mr. Strawman was about as lifelike as I could get him.

On Saturday morning I painted hair on Mr. Strawman as close to the color of Kordick's as I could, gave him a set of brown eyes and his mouth a pair of red lips. I glued a wooden match between the lips and let it hang.

On Monday I found an old broad-brim hat in the dump behind McCormick's and put it on Mr. Strawman. He was now ready to meet Mr. Kordick face to face.

I managed to get a couple of small paper bags from the kitchen and I was ready.

The moon was out that night and gave just enough light to make everything weird. For the first time the plan seemed silly, and for the first time I had doubts of its success. From that moment on I had to force myself to go through with it.

I slipped from my room along about twelve o'clock, scooted out to the barn, heaved Mr. Strawman to my shoulder and headed for Kordick's.

The house was dark and gloomy looking. I can't brag about my bravery for every time the wind whispered through the trees I was ready to head for home.

Suddenly I knew that unless everything went perfectly my plan would fall to pieces. Yet I was committed. I bore on. I plunged on, flinging my life against all reason into my plan. A new gnawing question bothered me: what did I expect to happen? To my surprise and consternation, I found I didn't know.

I propped Mr. Strawman behind a bush of waist-high barberry about thirty feet from Kordick's front porch. I fixed him so the broomstick gun aimed at the door.

I crept among the weeds near the porch, blew up one of the paper bags, twisted its neck, all the while fighting the urge to forget the plan and run, but I couldn't. I had to go through with it.

I dropped the pitch of my voice as low as possible and shouted, "Kordick! Kordick!"

I slammed my hand against the bag. It exploded like a shotgun blast.

There was a stir in the house.

I bellowed again. "Kordick, I'm after you!" I blew up the other bag and broke it.

The stillness of the night made the explosion seem fantastically loud.

There was a lot of commotion going on in the house by this time. I shouted once more, "Kordick, I'm after you!" and was about to bolt for home when the unexpected happened. The porch light flashed on.

If I ran I'd have to go through forty feet of light. I froze where I was. Perspiration soaked me. The front door squeaked open. I couldn't stay there for the weeds weren't thick enough to hide me completely. I slithered on my hands and knees close to the porch. The boards above creaked as someone stepped out. I saw an opening under the steps where a board had pulled loose. I wiggled through and hugged the musty ground.

Mousy Millie's voice sounded above me. "John," and a second later the porch shook with the impact of John Kordick.

"What's goin'—" Kordick's voice boomed and broke off suddenly and I figured he saw Mr. Strawman. More noise, thudding, scrambling, scraping and finally a house-shaking *wham!* as the front door was slammed shut.

I raised up wondering if I should make a run for it. I found a crack in the step, looked out and saw Mr. Strawman, wicked, sinister and surprisingly lifelike in the poor light, aiming the shotgun above my head toward the door. It was a sight, I want to tell you.

I started to wiggle backwards toward the hole, planning to make my getaway, when an upstairs window went up. I froze and stared at Mr. Strawman.

An explosion that seemed louder than any sound I had ever heard boomed above me. Mr. Strawman tilted slightly when buckshot smashed into his chest. His hat sailed off. A fraction of time passed and a second explosion roared in the night. Mr. Strawman wavered sidewards and went down behind the bushes.

John Kordick yelled hoarsely, "I got 'im!" The window slammed shut.

There was more noise coming from inside the house. I heard the distinct sounds of John ringing the phone; heard his voice high with excitement shouting words I couldn't quite make out.

Again I thought of running but couldn't muster up the courage to make the break. The gun that sent Mr. Strawman tumbling could do the same to me, and John Kordick wouldn't hesitate, so I lay under the porch, sweaty, trembly, yet as cold as though I were lying naked in a snowdrift.

Maybe fifteen minutes went by. It seemed like the longest spell I had ever come across. A car sounded in the distance. A few moments later it skidded into the driveway.

Gravel scattered. Brakes slammed on. A car door

opened. Gus Lance shouted, "Open up, Kordick! We're here!"

There was shuffling and Gus said, "Come on, Clarence."

Clarence was Gus' assistant in times of emergency. He was an oafish sort of man, about bright enough to run his gas station.

The two men walked into my range of vision. Clarence, yawning considerably, was barefoot and was tucking his shirt inside his trousers. Gus was shorter than Clarence; quick, alert and without fear. He had been one of the toughest fighters the United States had in France during the war, and had been decorated three different times for action beyond the call of duty.

Gus called again. By this time they were at the bottom of the steps and a second later they thumped above me.

The front door opened and Kordick stepped out on the porch. His voice was loud and boastful. "I'm glad you fellows come. I shot a man. I shot him in self-defense."

"What happened, Kordick?" Gus asked with no friendliness in his voice.

"Me and Millie was sleepin'. A shotgun blast woke me up. I sat on the edge of the bed for a minute and another shot rang out. Somebody shouted, 'John Kordick, I'm after you! I'm gonna gun you down.' First off I thought it was a joke, but I didn't recognize the voice so I hauled on my clothes. That guy was outside here shoutin' all the while, threatenin' me and Millie. Drunk, that's what he musta been. Drunk. I come downstairs and lit the porch light, come out, and there was this man standin' there bold as brass reloadin' his shotgun. I called out, 'What do you want?' He hollers back, 'I want money. All you got.' I told him to get off the place and let me go to sleep. What's he do but fires the shotgun at the roof of the house sayin', 'I'm warnin' ya, Kordick, the next blast will go between your eyes if I don't get what I want.'

"I ducked back into the house, got my gun and came out again. I told him I'd give him three to get off my place. I counted three, aimin' slow-like to give him a chance to get

66

away. While I was counting he's raisin' his gun. I didn't give him a chance to shoot. I shot twice, aimin' for his chest and down he went. He's lyin' yonder there, behind them bushes.''

Gus and Clarence came down the steps over my head and moved toward the bushes a little slow and cautious-like. Clarence had a flashlight and Gus had pulled out his revolver. Kordick was shouting directions but not following after the men.

"Not them first bushes on the right, but them barberry bushes on the left. He ought to be lying right behind them."

Gus reached the spot first and took the flashlight from Clarence. He sucked in his breath sudden-like. "Yup, here he is.''

The two men edged forward inch by inch with the beam of the flashlight probing the shadows.

John Kordick paced across the porch with his bare feet slapping the floor. Gus handed the flashlight to Clarence. "Hold this for me.''

Kordick called, "Do you know who it is?''

"Nope," Gus called back. "He's face down. Here, Clarence, give me a hand. We'll roll him over.''

The two men hunkered over and wrestled with Mr. Strawman for a minute. There was quite a bit of whispering between the two before Gus stood up, slipped his revolver back into its holster and called, "Do you have any idea who you shot, John?''

"Nope. To my knowledge, I never seen him before.''

"Did he have a high or deep voice?''

"Deep; deeper than most men.''

"And he was planning to rob you?''

"Yup, like I said, he said he'd kill me if I didn't give him money.''

"He'll never rob you, John. Don't worry about that. He's as dead as any man could be.''

John's voice held a trace of uncertainty. "I was in my rights, wasn't I, Gus? Shootin' a man on my front lawn, cussin' me and threatenin' Millie?''

67

Clarence stood up with a funny smirk on his face and said in his drawly, slow way. "Don't you worry none, John. If a man comes around talking big talk like that I'd say you had a right to lay him low, wouldn't you, Gus?"

"I sure would. I'da done the same thing myself."

John seemed relieved and he went on heaping one barefaced lie on another, braggin' all the time about his bravery. "When I first seen him he was out by the road; he kept comin' closer and closer. All the time he was wavin' the shotgun and demanding money. Isn't that right, Millie?"

A mousy little voice answered, "I guess so, John."

Kordick called, "Chief, will I go to trial for this?"

"Oh, I doubt it," Gus said easily, "but, Kordick, you'd better come down here and view the remains. Maybe you could help in identifying him."

The steps creaked and sagged. Kordick's elephantlike legs came into view, then his back and his neck shining purple-red in the porch light, the top of his head scraggly-haired and altogether an unpretty sight.

"You had plenty of courage, Kordick," Gus said, "shootin' a man armed with a gun like he has."

"I needed courage," John said. "I don't like this kind of stuff but when a man pushes me I don't sit still for it."

Clarence had turned the flashlight off and Kordick stooped over a little, peering behind the bushes. "Light's sorta bad for me to see anything."

"Hold on," Gus said, "we'll pull him out in the light."

I got a glimpse of Mr. Strawman when Gus and Clarence pulled him out on the path. He sure was a mess. His face wasn't bad, but the shotgun had ripped the coat into shreds and tufts of hay were sticking out of a couple dozen holes.

"What's this?" John whispered hoarsely.

"Now don't feel too bad, Kordick. This is the man you shot," Gus said in mock sympathy.

Clarence said in his slow, dopey way, "Now, Mr. Kordick, do you know him? Did you ever see him before?"

Kordick stared, befuddled, bewildered, and beaten. "That ain't no man. It's just a scarecrow."

"Yup, Kordick. I reckon you're right. Now tell us, what really happened?"

"I told the truth, I—" Kordick started, then he fell to stuttering, "I—I—I—well—well—well."

Gus sure was enjoying himself. He pulled a pad from his pants pocket and a stub of a pencil from his shirt. "Now, Kordick, go over that conversation you had with him again." He laughed.

Clarence laughed. Clarence didn't laugh bold like Gus. He wasn't looking at Kordick at all, but looking up at the moon, and off to the road, and down to Mr. Strawman.

"It looks to me, John, like you've been took."

Kordick whined, "Look here, fellows, you won't bother to mention this, will you?" He called to Millie, "Get my wallet, Millie. It's under the mattress in the bedroom. Bring it here." He looked back to the men, "Chief, Clarence, what's it worth to keep your mouth shut?"

"Oh, I don't know," Gus said in an easy sort of way.

"Would fifty dollars apiece help you to forget this?"

Gus couldn't help but laugh, "You attempting to bribe an officer of the law?"

"A hundred dollars apiece." You could tell Kordick was feeling sick. "A hundred dollars is a lot of money. If I give it to you, you've gotta promise—you've gotta promise never to say nothin'."

Mousy Millie came down the steps so quietly I never heard her. She wore a raggedy bathrobe and her hair was wound up in a kerchief. Kordick took the bulging wallet, opened it, and held it up to the light.

"Hold on," Gus said. "Kordick, you ought to know better than to think I'd take a bribe. Your call came into the police station officially tonight and as Southfield's Chief of Police, I'll have to put this on record."

Kordick's attitude changed. He shoved the wallet into his pocket. "You men let this get out and I'll guarantee you'll regret it!"

Gus snapped, his voice hard and clear, "Kordick, you've played the part of a fool tonight. Take your medicine.

69

I could easily report you for attempting to bribe an officer, and I could report you for threatening an officer. You called us. We came. It wasn't our doing. Now, come on, Clarence, let's put the deceased in the car for evidence.''

Kordick followed the men as they carried Mr. Strawman, pleading, attempting to bribe, and threatening. But Gus and Clarence left without another word.

Kordick and Millie returned to the house. The light went out. I don't know when I've ever been so satisfied at getting back at somebody. Getting back at George Hostler was keen, but nothing compared to this.

I stayed under the porch for twenty minutes, and when the moon slipped behind a cloud I skedaddled for home and fell asleep in no time.

CHAPTER 6

THE GOOD FEELING carried over into the next morning until about ten o'clock when the phone rang. Mama answered it. Of course I listened in on one side of the conversation.

"Hello?"

Pause.

"Oh, hello, Arnie!"

Pause.

"Yes, I think Jerry could come at eleven. What's the matter, are you sick?"

A long pause.

"Oh, I see. It sounds like it was exciting."

A short pause.

"Well, I can't say I feel too sorry for Mr. Kordick."

Pause.

"Well, if Mr. Kordick's mad at the chief, I'd hate to be in the chief's shoes."

A pause.

"Well, all right, Arnie, I'll send Jerry up."

"What was that all about?" I asked as soon as Mama hung up the phone.

"It seems someone played a trick on John Kordick, and Gus Lance is spreading it all over town. Arnie's afraid trouble might come. He wants you at the store so he can be free if necessary."

It didn't take me long to dress and light out for the store. Arnie was standing at the door when I arrived, munching the end of a roll of summer bologna and looking at Police Headquarters above the gas station.

He stepped aside as I entered.

"What's the matter?" I asked, noticing an unusually big crowd of men on the benches in front of Lucy's place.

"The chief is carrying a practical joke too far. If he keeps it up I figure there's goin' to be a pack of trouble."

A prickly feeling touched the base of my spine and jumped up my back and spread across my shoulders. "What happened?" I asked innocently.

"It's sort of hard to know," Arnie said. "One thing's for sure, Kordick's story and Gus' story don't line up. According to Gus, somebody rigged up a scarecrow and got John to shoot it. He thought he had shot a real man and called Gus in on it.

"John claims, on the other hand, that there were men that did threaten him and they had the straw man as a decoy. So who knows what?

"Apparently Kordick tried to bribe the chief and Clarence and when that didn't work he threatened to beat them up. Gus and Clarence have managed to spread the word around to let everybody know about the incident."

"It sounds exciting," I put in, feeling pleased.

"There's been a good deal of laughter, I'll say that," Arnie commented dryly.

The words popped out of my mouth before I thought what I was saying, "That John Kordick had it coming to him."

"Right enough. He deserves it and a lot besides. People ain't had much of a chance to catch Kordick over a barrel. They're taking advantage of it."

"What's the chief going to do?"

Arnie frowned, "I'd say he's done enough by just talking, but he and Clarence have announced they're going to put the body of the deceased, meaning the shot-up scarecrow, on view for the public to see at three o'clock this afternoon."

Arnie's frown shaded into a look of worry. "The chief's carrying this thing too far. Kordick, plus liquor, ain't a combination to fool with and he's been fortifying himself considerably. He's heard what the chief's planning to do and he's mad. I don't especially want Kordick for a friend, but I sure wouldn't want him for an enemy."

"Why is Gus carrying it so far?"

Arnie bit into the bologna and chewed it for a while. "He's got reason enough, I'll admit that. When Gus was in the army during the war his father died. The farm was to go to Gus. John was tax collector at the time and he also had a mortgage on the Lance place. Well, to make a long story short, when Gus came home a year and a half later he found that the farm that had been in the family for three generations had been taken over by Kordick. It was a sticky sort of a deal and dishonest, there was no question about that. Gus tried for two or three years to get the farm back but he failed. He ain't forgot it and I figure he's gonna make the most of this."

"Can't say that I blame him much."

"Can't blame the other people for feeling good about it either. 'Most everybody's felt Kordick's pinch and they're anxious to laugh at him." I winced when Arnie said the word, 'pinch,' for my ear was still as tender as a toothache. "Kordick'll fight back," Arnie went on. "I'll guarantee he's sorry he ever made that phone call."

Business was lively and every conversation circled around Mr. Kordick and Mr. Strawman. No one felt sorry for Kordick and most everyone was glad Gus was playing it up.

Miss Perry, who had been my eighth grade teacher, pushed through the doorway and entered the store.

I'm going to say some funny things now but every last one of them is true. When that lady, or girl, because she wasn't that much older than I, came into any place right off it brightened the place up 500 percent. She didn't have to say anything, a body was just so glad to see her he perked up. That made the eighth grade, for me, about as interesting as any grade could ever be. There were times, a heap of them, when I'd get to looking at her when maybe she was teaching history, and not even know she was teaching history.

Everybody was surprised when Jane Perry came back to

teach after college. Arnie said it a hundred times if he'd said it once, "That girl could go any place she wanted to and do anything she had a mind to and make it big, but here she is, giving that pretty life of hers to drilling information into the hollow-headed bumpkins that won't know what to do with it after they get it."

Fat Lucy liked Miss Perry, too. More than once when they were both in the store Fat Lucy would say, "Jane, you're wasting your time. You'll dry up in this burg." She was always after her to quit teaching.

I didn't follow that and I figured Miss Perry would never dry up. Why that girl could play first base like she was born there, and run—she was so quick I was hard put to catch her. There were other things, too, about her worth mentioning, like being adventuresome. Back when I was in her grade we'd go on a "field trip" once a week and we'd poke under stones along the creek beds and explore thickets and woods, and it was surprising how much stuff she knew. I never saw her flinch when something unexpected came about, like seeing a water snake or a muskrat.

Well, she came into the store, white-bloused, red-skirted, with her hair sort of messed up by the breeze but looking that natural it was nicer that way than if it were perfectly combed.

"Hi, there, Jerry!"

"Howdy, Miss Perry," I said, feeling as comfortably warm as a log on a fireplace.

"I've never seen our town quite so happy," she said to Arnie. "It's almost like carnival time."

"I'm worried," Arnie grumbled.

"It's a pity," Miss Perry said, "that Mr. Kordick has the genius to bring so much delight to people by making a fool of himself."

"Look, Jane," Arnie said seriously, "if I were you, I'd go offer Gus a little free advice and tell him to cut this out."

"Gus is old enough to know what he wants to do," Miss Perry shot right back in a tone that was surprising, for it gave me the idea that she didn't think much of him, and a tone I'd

74

never heard her use before. I looked at her quick-like and what I saw on her face wasn't anything like the tone in her voice. That was a real puzzler and I couldn't do a thing about working it out in my mind.

"Suit yourself," Arnie said, "but it just may be that Gus has tied into something here bigger than he thinks."

All the while we were talking more cars and trucks were filling the parking spaces and by 2:45 there were more people milling around than I'd ever seen before except at the fireworks display on the Fourth of July.

Lucy's place was doing a booming business. There wasn't a bench seat vacant and men were waiting around the door for a chance to get in.

Arnie left the store about ten minutes to three, saying as he went out, "I'm going to try to talk to Gus once more. Keep yourself busy."

I kept myself busy all right, watching the crowd, and I was some surprised to see as many womenfolk and children as men. The excitement was lively. It was more than lively. There was a holiday spirit about the whole thing and as the minutes passed I found it hard to stay in the store.

Finally I couldn't stand it any longer, for the activity was increasing around the door that led up to the police station and, like chickens flocking to cracked corn, people moved toward this point.

I left the store and became one of the mob. John Kordick's name was on everybody's lips. Mr. Strawman had sure done his job. It was real satisfying to hear what the people were saying, although the stories being passed around were as far from the truth as they could be.

"Can't understand," one woman with a baby in her arms said shrilly, "why that Kordick ain't in jail. No tellin' what he's likely to do, bein' a killer. I'm just glad it ain't one of the townsfolk he done in."

A boy, maybe seven, was downright gleeful, "Mama, Mama!"

"Hush," his mother said, because he was interrupting a conversation she was having with another woman about

75

Mousy Millie being sick and nigh unto death from the whole thing.

"Mama, are they going to shoot him?"

"Hush, I told you."

"Mama, do you think they'll shoot him?"

"Hush."

"Maybe hang him? I hope they hang him. That'd be more like it. Hangin's better for a crook anyway."

"Hush," his mother said, unmindful of what he was saying, and she went on talking about Mousy Millie.

"Hangin' ought to be excitin'. Pow!" The boy leaped, draped his head forward, eyes bulging, mouth wide open and tongue hanging out.

"Hush," the woman said and glanced at the boy to see him at the most gruesome stages of hanging. She let out a scream. "Olan! What's the matter? Olan!"

The boy's imitation of the hanging act ceased and he said blandly, "Nothin'."

"Do you feel sick?"

"Nope."

I don't know how it ended, because the crowd thickened and when I say thickened, I mean just that and the closer to the police station we moved the thicker it got.

I spotted a couple of people in an elm tree and figured that was as good a place as any to see the show, so I wiggled my way up and managed to get a dandy spot on a low limb. It wasn't a minute too soon, either, because the tree got plenty crowded and inside of two minutes there wasn't enough room left for a hummingbird to settle.

The noise silenced near the station and the silence quickly spread to the outer fringes. The people closest to the door were peering through it and suddenly backed off and a moment later Gus emerged and climbed on a chair.

A wave of applause went up and there was a lot more of it than for any speech our mayor ever made. Gus was dressed fit to kill; brass badge glistened in the sun, blue hat tilted in a rakish way with the visor almost covering one eye, uniform clean pressed and black shoes shiny as wet asphalt.

He held up his hands like King Tut himself and a hush came over the crowd.

When it was quiet enough he said loud and solemn-like, "Fellow-citizens, it's not often we have an event this important in Southfield. Murders are not easy to come by. I checked the record books this morning and the last time such an event [he said event like *e-*vent and made it very important sounding] occurred was back in the month of July of 1874. Not many of our townspeople alive today were present at that time, so I'll take this opportunity to go back in history and bring you up to date.

"Seems two of our ancestors, both men, one by the name of Hillegus and the other by the name of Bartlett, were courting the same gal, namely Johanna Peters."

A wave of laughter swept over the crowd.

"Naturally," Gus went on, "some of the facts are a little hazy, but it does appear that Johanna was especially free with her promises. Why that girl did a plumb foolish thing and when those two men popped the question she popped right back and said yes to both of them. She went so far as to give Mr. Hillegus a date for marriage in July and a date in August to Mr. Bartlett. You'll have to admit this created a tacky problem."

Gus pointed to the church across the square and said, "The July date came, the tenth I think it was, and Johanna and Mr. Hillegus were duly wed.

"It turned out to be an extremely short marriage, for when the bride and groom started down them church steps the August suitor, Mr. Bartlett, showed up and with one shot in the heart he terminated the life of Mr. Hillegus. The bereaved bride bent over her lover and with sweet tears of sadness said good-bye."

At Gus' last words the crowd really tuned up and gave him a walloping big cheer.

The way Gus had told the story hadn't made it sound like the truth, but it was just about accurate in every detail. Papa's papa, my grandpapa, told me the whole story before he died. He knew it was truth, he'd been there and had seen the whole thing. And you know something, that Mr. Bartlett went to prison for the murder and that girl, Johanna, waited for him and when he got out she married him. They didn't stay around town long and after they left no one ever heard from them again, which wasn't any great loss, if you ask me.

Gus was talking again. "Now the years have spun by and Southfield can look with pride to another milestone, to another murder—or was it a murder? This will be determined by you as you hear the facts of the case. Let me tell you about it. Last night darkness fell upon our community and none of us thought that a desperate criminal was lurking somewhere in the shadows, waiting for an opportunity to move against one of our most notable citizens, John Kordick."

A derisive laugh split the air.

"Mr. Kordick lay on his bed peaceful, innocent and never having hurt anyone."

The sound that came from the crowd was laughter, but there was an ugliness about it that I'd never heard before. I knew John Kordick was hated but never realized the deepness of the thing.

Gus was enjoying himself. He went on: "The figure emerged from the shadows and stood in front of John Kordick's home; stealthy, determined and dangerous. In his possession was a gun and the will to use it against a man; not a little man, mind you, but a very big one."

Another snort of laughter.

"Mr. Strawman," Gus went on, and I almost fell out of the tree thinking how I'd used that name from the beginning and that I'd never mentioned it to anybody, and for a moment wondering whether Gus was a mind reader, and then passing it off because how could he know my mind? "Mr. Strawman, for this was the culprit's name, hurled a challenge at John Kordick and John rose to the occasion. After conversing with Mr. Strawman at some length, and giving Mr. Strawman opportunity after opportunity to escape with his life, he raised his own shotgun and with cool detachment rid our town of the menace. Mr. Kordick then proceeded to call in the law, namely Clarence and myself."

I wondered what that crowd would have done if I had shouted that I had been at the root of the whole thing. I reckoned I could have run for mayor and made it pretty easy, and I felt a little cheated losing out that way.

Gus went on, "We, indeed, are indebted to John Kordick for his bravery. As always, he was dedicated to maintaining tranquility in our town at any price."

More ugly laughter.

"While we have a corpse, I'm sure you'll agree that John Kordick must go free, content to realize that he has whatever respect we can give him for his actions. I trust he'll live with this in his heart for years to come and walk with pride among us."

A roar of laughter.

"You, fellow townspeople, are here, I hope, not out of morbid curiosity to see the contents of the coffin, but rather to pay tribute to John Kordick. Some have expressed a desire to hear Mr. Kordick speak on the subject and explain in detail all that occurred. I am sorry to have to disappoint you. Whether it's humility, modesty, or shyness, I don't know, but for some reason Mr. Kordick is not present."

Gus turned to the door with an elegant gesture and called, "Clarence, these folks are anxious to pay their last respects. Proceed with the proceedings."

The crowd surged forward. Gus shouted, "Stand back! You'll all have an opportunity."

A couple of bums from Lucy's place produced wooden sawhorses and set them up in front of Gus. Clarence sort of stumbled out the door. He was dressed like a bank president, or maybe even better. It was the first time I'd ever seen him dressed in anything but his greasy overalls and it was surprising to see what clothes did for him; black suit with long tails 'most down to the back of his knees, gray-striped pants, white necktie, white flower in his lapel and a stovepipe hat. He caused a considerable stir.

Following Gus came four other men dressed like him, only with white gloves and they were hefting a coffin; a real one. I'll have to say this for Clarence, he did it big. He directed the carrying of that coffin to the sawhorses and then stood at one end straight and proud-like.

Gus held up his hands again and in a mournful, singsongy voice said, "Before we view the deceased, I'd like to remind you of the seriousness of this occasion. We want no levity. Womenfolk are asked not to weep for too long a time at the coffin. Children under twelve must be accompanied by their parents. If any of you are aware of the location of Mr. Strawman's relatives let us know, for up to date we've not been able to find his kinfolk and we would like to inform them of their loss."

Clarence, acting like he owned the town, walked stiffly to the front of the coffin and slowly raised the lid, and there was Mr. Strawman stretched out with his busted-in chest and with the broomstick gun lying beside him. I never saw a crowd so anxious to carry on, and I don't ever remember hearing so much laughing. They filed past Mr. Strawman. Some of the men shook his hand. Men and women alike made believe dabbing tears from their eyes. Fat Lucy really set everybody going when she gave a wail, bent over and kissed Mr. Strawman's cheek, and the look on Gus' face was a sight to see; like he'd just gotten five thousand dollars he hadn't expected.

There was a stir up above me in the branches and I heard somebody say, "Ain't that John Kordick comin' down the road?"

Then there was a shout from the top of the tree, "John Kordick's a comin'!"

At first no one paid heed, but after a couple of seconds a dozen voices were shouting, "John Kordick's on his way!"

Now it's sure peculiar to see how things can change a crowd's mood. As more and more people heard that John was coming the quieter things got and a heap of folks seemed to be awful anxious to be some distance from the coffin.

I wiggled around until I could look through the leaves, and sure enough, John Kordick was coming and fast. He lumbered down the center of the road and weaved from side to side like he didn't know which way to go next; unshaven, sweaty, match hanging from his lips, barn boots muddy, a couple of strands of hair hanging down and plastered to his cheeks by sweat. His head was down with his eyes staring at the road and he cradled a shotgun in the crook of his left arm, and his right hand was fussing with the trigger.

He paused in front of Arnie's store and came on again, slowly now and deliberately and not looking at anything particular, but just straight ahead and downish. I'll tell you something, that crowd had silenced off so you could hear John's boots scuffing against the pavement and you could hear his breathing too.

When John reached a point opposite the coffin he bore right and headed for the thickest mass of people. My, there was a scurry and rustle as folks tried to clear a way for him, he never missing a step and the path opening up just about three feet ahead of him. He passed underneath me and I made out plain as day the blood veins crisscrossing his almost-bald head. His jowls flared out purplish-like and the back of his neck didn't seem like any neck at all, but a great red roll of fat speckled with bristles.

He marched straight to the coffin, glanced at Mr. Strawman, then looked up. He raised a thick finger and pointed at Gus. "I warned you! Don't never say I didn't warn you!"

Those words were enough to chill a snowflake but Gus never batted an eye. A satisfied smile turned the corner of his lips. "Mr. Kordick," he said very formally, "I'm only doing you justice, giving you your due reward," which seemed like a funny thing to say, but I didn't have time to think it through, for Kordick turned toward the crowd.

I can't put down everything he said. Some of the words weren't the kind nice people use, but here's part of it:

"You're all a yellow pack of skunks! True enough, I was took last night. I don't know who done it, but I'll find out. When I do, you'll have a real murder on your hands, mark my words. And don't think I won't find out. I will."

The match bobbled from one side of Kordick's mouth to

the other. While he was talking his voice rose. "I don't know what Gus has been telling you, but it's a pack of dirty lies."

Suddenly he took the match from between his lips and swept the head against his pants leg. "You fools!" he shouted. "You fools!" The match sprang into flame and Kordick dropped it on Mr. Strawman's chest. The hay burst into flames. The people who were closest fell back, shoving against the people who were behind them and the people behind pressed forward to try to see better what was going on.

Kordick watched the fire until it had pretty much reduced Mr. Strawman to ashes and was starting on the coffin. Then he swung around, put his head down, and strode bulllike toward the thickest part of the mob again. I'll tell you something, that crowd stirred pretty lively and everyone watched as John Kordick stomped down the middle of the road toward his place.

Clarence, who had been standing stiff-like nearby, jumped toward the coffin and slammed down the lid. A belch of smoke flew out and for a few minutes the fire seemed extinguished. The crowd silenced, sobered, studied the coffin.

A blue edge of flame shot out from under the lid. Another, and another caught, looking a little like an inverted waterfall. It didn't take long for the entire coffin to break out.

Lucy shrilled, "Look out, them gas tanks could go up any minute!"

That did it. The crowd broke, turned and re-formed in a huge circle. Clarence and Gus hadn't moved; Clarence, standing there oxlike, and Gus still on the chair, contented. Gus said, "There's no danger."

The coffin sagged in the middle and finally folded in on itself, making a nice neat fire between the wooden horses.

I climbed out of the tree and worked my way through the mob to the store.

Arnie came in some time later; grim, but he didn't say much, for business turned brisk. Candy, ice cream and soda pop were our main items. It was a gay thing to be part of that, and especially satisfactory knowing you were a cause of it all.

82

How people talked! Going over every detail and adding a heap that never happened. The only sobering thing I heard, and I heard it way too many times, were the words, "When Kordick finds out who done it, that'll be the end of him."

That wasn't too comforting. There was a lot of speculation as to who had done it. I guess half the men in town were blamed at one time or another and a couple of them let on they knew more about the thing than they were saying.

Along about six Gus came in, still polished fit to kill, and content. "Gus," Arnie said reprovingly, "now you've got it started again, how do you aim to stop it?"

Gus laughed, "I don't intend to stop it, Arnie. There's a heap of satisfaction in a thing like this."

"You've kicked a sleeping dog, Gus. You got 'im snarling again."

"I'm not afraid of Kordick," Gus said, and you could tell he wasn't. "And he'd never lay a finger on me, anyway."

"I wasn't thinking of you, Gus, but that scarecrow has put Kordick in a ridiculous light. He's bound and determined to find out who did it. He'll find out, too. He'll go over every person in town and gnaw away at the facts he's got, and he'll come up with the answer, and once he finds out, there won't be any stopping him." Arnie looked up suddenly, "Gus, did you do it?"

Gus sobered, "I wish I could take credit for it, Arnie. Whoever did it was clever. I don't know how they manged it, but it took sheer genius. I'll admit this, if Kordick finds out who did do it, I'd advise the party to walk only in the daytime and to always be with somebody."

"You got any ideas who might've?"

"Nope, but there's enough candidates to make the field pretty broad."

I just hope he doesn't have a family," Arnie ended the sentence with a weak little laugh.

Guess how I felt standing there listening to my death notice. Just guess how I felt. I got to quivering so badly I sorta had to hold onto the candy case and my knuckles were whitish, I was holding on so hard. And sweat; I never just plain sweat the way I did then; cold and clammy it was.

Suddenly I had to get out of there, that's all there was to it. I had to get out of there. I headed for the door, not even taking my apron off; not even thinking about my apron, but just goin'.

Arnie hollered at me, "You ain't goin' home?"

I hollered right back, "I am so, it's twenty after six." And I went, too.

I busted into the kitchen letting the screen door slam like Mama doesn't like it to slam and ran head-on into Lillie. First off she spotted the apron. "How come?" she asked.

"None of your business!" I shouted. "If I want to wear an apron I'll wear an apron! Right now I just feel like wearing an apron," which was a pretty ridiculous thing to say when you think of it. But what was I going to do, tell her the real reason?

Ordinarily Lillie would have kept at it, but tonight she didn't because she was so plum curious as to what had happened she fired questions quicker than a flock of blackbirds going south, and Mama wasn't too far behind her.

"Allie called," Allie being Mrs. McCormick, "and said there was quite a to do at the center of town."

"Uh huh."

"Don't stand there like a dope," Lillie shrilled. "What happened?"

"Oh, Gus and Clarence burned a scarecrow. I'm hungry."

"Why did they burn a scarecrow?"

"Oh, I guess they just like to do things like that."

"Jerry," Mama said with a note of warning. "We missed out on all the excitement. Allie told us a lot of funny things. Now I've never known her to fib, but they're so strange I've a mind to know just what happened. Now you talk up and answer our questions."

"Yes, Mama." And I did, and every question made me sicker and it didn't help any when Lillie kept saying, "Just wait 'til John Kordick finds out who pulled that one."

Doing evening chores was a relief but when I brought the milk into the house Lillie went at it again and by the time I went to bed I was plain tuckered out.

I guess I slept for a little while, but along about twelve I was awakened by Rusty's barking. Rusty had a heap of different kinds of barks: a friendly one for members of the family; another friendly one, but a little different for people he knew; an unfriendly one for strangers; and another unfriendly one, but different for dogs he didn't like; and a kind of a friendly, unfriendly one for the animals: coons, skunks and the like who came sniffing around our chicken coop.

Being half asleep made it hard for me, right off, to know what kind of bark Rusty was using. At first I figured it was his bark for strangers and that jolted me, and when I woke up enough to know it was his animal bark I was so disturbed I couldn't get to sleep. I tossed and I turned, fussed with the pillow, pulled the sheet over my head, wrestled with the blanket and kept thinking about what was going to happen when John Kordick caught me, and I had no doubt that he would.

The clock downstairs struck one and it was like a knife cutting into my most tender parts, for at that moment I thought of Mr. Wade and those plaguing pamphlets he had given Arnie, especially the one entitled, "Where Will You Spend Eternity, In Heaven or Hell?"

Those words seemed to hang like a billboard in front of my eyes, and the answer to that question banged into my mind and was about as uncomforting as seven boils on your tongue.

"You're going to hell," I murmured, and I was sweating again, but some colder than before. The more I tried to kick that thought out of my mind, the more it dug in like a drill, saying the same thing over and over again, and it kept on going until I heard the clock strike two.

I got up and closed the window and locked it, and set Rusty barking his friendly bark with the noise I made. I put the sheet, the blanket and the pillow over my head when I got back into bed and somehow I fell asleep. I didn't hear three, or four o'clock chime, but at five I was awake with dawn coming through the window and that plagued question was as bright and fresh as it had been when it first hit me and I took special notice of the sunrise, the wren's song, the garden patch and the barn, figuring it would be the last time I would see those dear things.

CHAPTER 7

IT DIDN'T TURN OUT to be an easy day any way I looked at it. Mama and Lillie pounced on me at breakfast with more questions, and at the store it was worse, with everybody talking. I knew everything that was said could not be true, but if only one-hundredth of it were true, it was worse than I thought.

I won't put down all the conversations, but just part of them. Here's about how it went:

About six-thirty the previous evening John Kordick stomped into town staggering drunk. He carried the shotgun and went from house to house carrying on something fierce, asking people if they knew who had done it.

"It was awful," Mrs. Baker said, "him smellin' like raw whiskey and sweatin' so much I declare you coulda wrung water outa his shirt, and he barges right into my livin' room with them filthy barn boots on, and scarin' the kids, and sayin', 'Where's yer man?' and me sayin', 'He won't be here 'til nine o'clock,' and him sayin', 'Guess I'll wait.' And he sat on the couch messin' with that shotgun all the while he was waitin' with a handkerchief so dirty I wouldn't use it to clean a barn window, and him not usin' it only to rub the barrel of that gun, but every now and then wipin' off his lips with it, and wipin' his forehead, yet. An' when my Sheldon comes through the door innocent and unsuspectin'-like, and John gettin' up off the couch pointin' the shotgun at him and sayin', 'Did you put that there scarecrow in front of my house?' and my Sheldon almost fallin' over, him bein' as

87

timid as he is and sayin', 'No,' and John bargin' out sayin' as how he'd find that jokester if it's the last thing he did. An' me and the kids bawlin' somethin' awful after he left.

Guess how I felt!

Mrs. Drummond had the liveliest story. "It was past nine, and me bein' tired I went to bed early." Mrs. Drummond is always tired and anybody could see why. She weighed upwards of two hundred and fifty and was only maybe five feet. Maybe that's stretching it a little bit, but she is awful big.

"Well, I hear this pounding on the door and I think it's Jake, and him supposed to have been home at five for supper, and me having it ready at that time, and him not coming, so I figures a lesson I'll learn him. So I don't get up right away, and he keeps right on pounding so finally I gets up and goes through the kitchen, stopping just long enough to get a glass full of water and I goes outside and around the house and I shoulda known right off it wasn't Jake, 'cause Jake isn't so big, but I didn't think, and I sneaks up and throws the water. I knew it wasn't Jake then. It was John Kordick and that water takes him so sudden he pulls on the trigger, because he's carryin' a shotgun and he cut down one of my rosebushes just as neat. It's there for anybody to see, and anyway, my Annie [Annie's a girl about five] turns on the porch light and there I was embarrassed and scared, too in my—in my—night-gown, petrified and I couldn't move, and that man asking me if I knew who done that trick. Just then Jake pulls in the driveway, and my Jake's got spunk, and he puts that John Kordick off the place."

And so it went all day. How much was true a body couldn't tell, but there was plumb nothing that gave me any comfort.

At five-thirty I worked my way to the back of the store about filled up with what I could take. When Arnie was waiting on a customer I slipped out.

We were just finishing supper that night, I guess it was about seven, when Papa came home.

I wanted to hug him, I wanted to kiss him, I wanted to

climb right inside of him, I was that relieved. I never figured a person could be that glad to see a person, but I was, and I wanted him all to myself, but what with Lillie and Betsy and Mama, I had to stand off to one side.

"Hi, Jer!" he at last said to me. "I stopped at Arnie's to see if you were still at work. I hear you had a lot of excitement since I've been gone."

Lillie chimed in. "Mama and I wanted to go up, but we didn't want Betsy to see anything that wasn't nice, but Jerry saw it all."

"I'm sorry I missed out," Papa said. "It's not often we have a stir like that in town. Arnie seems to think the worst is yet to come."

"Why should Arnie be so upset about it? It's none of his affair." Lillie put in.

"Arnie has good sense," Papa said soberly, "and he's afraid Kordick is going to do something desperate to some innocent man. Clarence came into the store while I was there and he claims Kordick figures Jack Spear was in on the joke."

"Jack Spear!" Lillie snorted. "That jellyfish wouldn't dare do anything like that."

"Well, the coat on the scarecrow was the one Jack Spear had on his scarecrow, according to Clarence, so Kordick's jumping to the conclusion that Jack's his man."

That old ball of barbed wire rumbled down my throat and into my stomach, then rolled up again and sat just behind my tongue. I said weakly, "Any old fool could've swiped that scarecrow."

"True enough," Papa said, "but Kordick's acting so crazy now he's likely to jump at any straw to get revenge."

It was a task to act natural under those circumstances, especially with that same old sickness I'd had the night before developing plenty fast. Papa looked straight at me. "Jerry, I guess you've enjoyed a heap of satisfaction seeing Kordick fooled this way after what he did to you."

I had to say something, but what a job to say it easygoing and offhand-like. "Yessiree, Papa. I keep wishing I'd thought of that trick myself," which was about the whop-pingest big lie I had ever told.

Mama exclaimed, "Oh, Jerry! Don't you dare ever say a thing like that!" She turned to Papa, "Adam, you don't suppose John Kordick'll think Jerry had anything to do with it?"

I hung onto my fork like a drowning man.

Papa laughed, "Amy, forget your foolish fancies. Kordick has sense enough to know this isn't a boy's trick. It's been too well plotted and planned for that."

"Humph," Lillie snorted, snapping her fingers, "if I were John Kordick, I'd just sit down and figure out who hated me the most, and—" She snapped her fingers again. "I'd know who did it."

Papa said, "When you have as many enemies as John Kordick you'd likely have a heap to choose from."

That conversation dragged on, wallowing around Kordick for the whole meal.

After supper I played a few games of checkers with Papa and lost every one of them.

"What's the matter, son?" he asked. "You're pretty quiet tonight, and that's the first time in a year I won seven games in a row. Are you worrying about this Kordick case?"

Now there's a question for you! How was a body supposed to answer that? I fished around for a second and came up with, "I sure hope Jack Spear doesn't get hurt," which was the truth and it put Papa off.

Bed was about as comforting as trying to sleep on a rosebush that night, and I had a bunch of nightmares all ending with John Kordick running after me and gaining, with a big burning match in one hand and a shotgun in the other. It was enough to keep a body restless, and when dawn finally came I was more tuckered out than when I went to bed.

That day, Thursday, I wasn't in the store ten minutes before Arnie slipped into his shoes. I glanced through the front window and saw John Kordick shuffling up the steps. He wasn't a pretty picture and it's kind of hard to believe how a man could let himself look like that: shaggy-haired, shaggy-bearded, sweat-soaked shirt, with the top three buttons pulled off and spread out unsightly-like, beads of moisture hanging from his sagging lower lip, with a match dangling in one corner. One of his trouser legs was outside of his boot, while the other one was tucked in, and those trousers looked like he slept in the pigpen, which may not have been far from the truth from the way he smelled when he burst through the door. His suspenders seemed almost at the breaking point and the right shirttail was dangling free.

I had an awful hankering to break and run and I think I would have if Kordick had so much as glanced at me, but he didn't.

Arnie jumped right into him with a tone sharper than an ax. "John, you'd better get hold of yourself. You're actin' the part of a fool. Best thing you can do is forget about this thing."

John mumbled and right off I saw he was drunk—sodden drunk. "Ain't gonna forget 'til I find out."

"Forget it, and the people'll forget it, John. Keep remembering, and the people will keep remembering."

"You know who done it, don't you Arnie?"

Arnie snapped, "I don't, but if I did I wouldn't tell you."

"You know who done it," Kordick grunted. "Everybody does." Kordick thumped his hands, palm downward, on the counter and leaned over, "Spear done it, didn't he, Arnie?"

Arnie cracked the words out like pistol shots. "You're a fool, Kordick! You know Jack Spear better'n that."

"I seen that scarecrow in his garden."

"OK, so it was Jack's crow. Somebody swiped it."

"He done it," Kordick muttered. "I'll git 'im. I'll git 'im tonight."

Arnie jumped from his stool and rushed around the counter. Now Arnie's a heap bigger'n the average man, but Kordick was a good six inches taller and a hundred and fifty pounds heavier. That didn't stop Arnie. He grabbed hold of Kordick's shirt and gave a yank that almost upset John. "You fool! You go home and sober up and stay away from that blasted Lucy's. Do you hear me!''

Kordick raised his hands, thick-fingered, filthy, and put them on Arnie's chest and shoved.

Arnie fell backwards, hit the counter and went for Kordick again.

Kordick's fists were clenched. His head sagged forward and there was the oddest film dulling his eyes.

Arnie grabbed Kordick's suspenders, one in each hand, and said in a penetrating voice, ''John, I'm trying to help you. Whatever's happened to you, you've earned. You've pushed everybody too far. Now you've pushed me too far.''

Kordick's right arm was moving back, hamlike fist cocked. Arnie saw it. ''You lay a finger on me, Kordick.'' That's all he said, but it seemed to do something and Kordick dropped his hand to his side.

''Now get out of this store,'' Arnie said, ''and don't come back unless you're sober. I'm fed up.''

Kordick left, too; left and went straight over to Lucy's.

Arnie returned to the stool, kicked off his shoes and stared out at the sunbaked street.

About half-past four Kordick came out of Lucy's and shuffled down the center of the street toward home. Before he was out of sight Lucy came out and walked over to the store.

Lucy was about the unprettiest woman in the world: yellowish-gray hair all ascraggled, teeth missing, and those she had, stained considerably, dirty apron, and all around about as run-down as you'd want to see a woman.

''Arnie,'' she chirped, about as lively as a sparrow, ''you must've said some awful mean things to John. You hurt him awful deep.''

''What?'' Arnie roared disgustedly.

''He said once you were his best friend, but now you've turned agin' him.''

''If I was ever John Kordick's best friend I'd hate to know what his enemies think of him, and if I were you, Lucy, I'd kick him out of that place of yours.''

92

"Why, Arnie!" Lucy smirked. "Get rid of the best customer I have?" She noticed me. "Hello, Jerry Berry!"

She always called me that and I hated it. She made it sound like she was talking to a pampered puppy or a coddled cat. "You look peaked," she babbled on. "I'll bet Arnie's overworking you. How much does he pay you an hour?"

Arnie didn't give me a chance to answer. "Enough!" he snapped.

"If I know you, Arnie," Lucy's voice was sickly sweet, "you're cheating him left and right. There's not a boy in town works as hard as poor Jerry Berry does."

She turned to me again, "Jerry Berry, I'll give you twenty-five cents an hour if you come work for me."

Arnie was stirred up. "Cut out that nonsense, Lucy!"

Lucy didn't cut it out. She chirped right on. "I need an errand boy. Why, Jerry Berry, I could use you from eight o'clock in the morning 'til twelve o'clock at night. If you'd work all them hours it'd come to four dollars a day, and there's a heap of men in this town who aren't making that much."

Arnie was red-faced. "Lucy, cut it out! If Gus had any sense he'd run you out of town. Ninety-nine percent of all the trouble that busts loose starts right over there." He jerked a thumb toward her building. "It wouldn't surprise me one bit if that whole mess with Kordick wasn't hatched over in your back room."

"Could be." Lucy wagged her head knowingly. "Could be."

"Well, if you know anything about it, woman, you'd better keep your mouth shut."

Lucy said smugly, "Oh, I know about it, but I ain't the talkin' type."

"What?" Arnie exploded again.

"Now, Arnie," Lucy said peevishly, "I ain't, and I do know who did it."

"You're a lyin' woman," Arnie snorted.

Lucy didn't blink an eyelash. "You'll see. You'll see," she said knowingly.

I almost pitched flat on the floor. I sagged against the candy case.

Lucy turned to me. "Jerry Berry, you tell that real nice pappy of yours to pay me a call sometime. Tell him to come see what a very nice place I have. You ask him if you can't come work for me. You'll do that, won't you, Jerry Berry?" She paused, then babbled on, "Why, Jerry Berry, you look positively sickly. Is old Arnie really working you that hard?"

"Yes, ma'am," I murmured. "I mean—no, ma'am."

Arnie's self-control got out of hand. "Woman," he shouted, "what do you want? Give me your order or get out. And you let that boy alone, hear me? You want to ruin him like you've ruined everybody else that's listened to you?"

You would think Lucy would fight a thing like that. She didn't. She stood there with the silliest kind of grin on her face. "Why, Arnie, gettin' stirred up like this won't help your health none." She dug a list out of her apron pocket and gave it to him as cool as cool can be.

While Arnie filled the order he lectured, "I don't know what this town's coming to. My father would turn over in his grave if he knew what was going on now. Decency's plumb gone."

He wasn't reaching Lucy, though. She stood there with her hands on her hips watching Arnie and whistling a tune I'd never heard before. At first Arnie paid no heed but kept right on talking. Suddenly he stopped and the look on his face was a sight to see.

"Woman!" he shouted. "Woman!"

Lucy's whistling never missed a note.

Arnie hustled that order as quick as I'd ever seen him hustle any order and he slammed the items on the counter like he was aiming to break it into kindling. He poked the keys on the cash register furiously. "Seven dollars and twenty-seven cents!" he shouted when he finished, "and it's ashamed I am to take your dirty money."

She handed over a ten-dollar bill.

He counted out the change and said, "Woman, I pride myself on treating my customers with respect. There's a new

94

man in town name of Wade, a reformer. I'll direct him your way."

Lucy stuck the change into her apron pocket and hoisted the bag of groceries to her arms. Only then did she stop whistling. She winked at me and turned to Arnie. "I'd be happy to meet Mr. Wade. Send him over. I'd be happy to have you come over, too, sometime, Arnie. Sounds like both of you need a little enjoyment in life."

She winked at me again. "Jerry Berry, you look about petered out. Why, you're tremblin', child. Don't you let Arnie work you too hard. Now open the door for me."

I did, and she started to whistle again. Then off she went, leaving Arnie about as worked up as I'd ever seen him.

Arnie didn't have a chance to take off his shoes before Mr. Wade drove up. "Oh no! Two village idiots gone, and the third shows up. Must be about time I sold out and retired."

Mr. Wade entered, smiling and easygoing. "Hi, young man!" he said to me, and then to Arnie, "Mr. Beard, I have an errand to do. Here's my order, and if convenient, I'll pick it up about an hour from now." He laid the list on the counter, and as always, his hand went to his shirt pocket and pulled out another pamphlet. "There are some provocative thoughts here. Read it and tell me what you think."

Mr. Wade went to the door, not giving Arnie a chance to say anything, but he said plenty after Mr. Wade left. "Why is that man after me? Does he tackle Fat Lucy? Nosiree! Or Kordick? Nosiree! Does he tackle any of those bums over in front of Lucy's place? Nosiree! He tackles me." He looked at the pamphlet. "Seven Presuppositions Basic to Understanding Christianity." He read sarcastically, his voice unusually high-pitched and raw-like:

Man must presuppose that God exists. — Hebrews 11:6.

Man must presuppose the Bible is God's revelation of Himself. — Hebrews 1:1-3.

Man must presuppose that man's thinking is faulty. — 1 Corinthians 1:18-28.

Man must presuppose that God let man go his own way in sin. — Romans 1:2-24.

Man must presuppose that when anything seems to contradict the Bible it is simply because all the facts are not in view. — 1 Corinthians 4:5.

Man must presuppose that the only lasting things are the things he cannot see and that absolutely all the things he sees are temporary and will pass away. — 2 Corinthians 4:18.

Man must presuppose that faith in the Lord will bring more faith and that man must live by faith alone. — Romans 1:17.

I don't think Arnie was aware that I was present. He stopped reading aloud and looked at that pamphlet. I believe he read it at least three times, and although he was interrupted four times by customers, he kept at it.

Mr. Wade came back and picked up his order. "Did you get a chance to read that article?"

Arnie said shortly, "Sir, I'm a busy man. If I spent all my time reading everything people hand me, I'd go out of business within a week."

It didn't seem to bother Mr. Wade a bit. He paid his bill and left, and believe it or not, Arnie picked up that pamphlet again. It was about as much as I could stand, and although I wasn't feeling too gay, I began to whistle the same tune that Lucy had whistled just to see what would happen.

I had about gone on ten seconds when Arnie's head jerked up. "Boy," he said, "You're fired! Get out of here!"

That was more than I had counted on. I started to say something, but he cut me off. "Get!" he roared. "Nobody in my employ whistles that song!"

There was nothing I could do, but get, which wasn't what I wanted to do at all.

He glared at me, brittle and bitter.

I loafed along walking home until twenty after six, not wanting Mama to know I'd been fired.

Mama met me at the door. "Where have you been, Jerry? Arnie's called 'most twenty times. Claims you left the store before quitting time. You're to call him back. He sounded very upset.''

I rang him up and said, sort of weakly, "Arnie?"

"Jerry," and he did seem upset. "Why were you whistling that?"

"I don't know. It's just that I thought it was a catchy tune.''

"Do you know the words that go with it?"

"No.''

I could hear him take in a long, deep breath, and when he spoke again his voice was relieved. "Jerry, you come back and work for me tomorrow." There was a long pause before he continued, "Jerry, don't ever whistle that again.''

"Why!" I asked, feeling relieved, but curious.

Arnie said one word, "Filthy," and he said it with a note of finality that closed the door on the tune and I never did find out what disturbed him so. Yet afterwards I remembered that tune, note for note, and I kept trying to find out what the words were. That plagued thing ran through my mind like it was part of me.

Papa came home around seven-thirty and of course for the major part of the meal Lillie filled us in on the latest nonsense about the wedding. Finally there was a little break and I knifed in casually, "Someone came into the store today, said they'd give me twenty-five cents an hour if I'd work for them, could work about as many hours as I had a mind to, if you'd let me.''

"Take it," Lillie snapped.

"I could make almost twelve dollars any old week if I wanted to.''

"No one in town would pay a boy that much," Mama said.

"Sounds good, Jerry," Papa said. "Who made the offer?"

"Lucy," I replied. "She was in the store toda—"

It was a curious thing. Nobody said anything right off, but the change that came into that room was surprising. Lillie clapped her hand over her mouth as though I'd said a bad

97

word, and Mama sucked in her breath, sort of like the whistle on top of the volunteer fire department, and Papa chipped in by clearing his throat. *"Hurrump, hurrump,"* he groaned, and laid his fork ever so carefully beside his plate and studied his coffee cup as though it were a diamond he was seeing for the first time.

Finally he said, "You mean, *that* woman [he said the word *that* like a shot from a pistol] had the raw courage to offer a boy like you a job in a place like hers?"

"That's right, Papa."

"The answer is no!" he thundered. "Absolutely no!"

I wasn't exactly surprised at this reaction, but it was sort of pleasurable to see things stirred up so.

I went on, "Lucy said to tell you, Papa, that she'd like very much for you to come into her place sometime. She says it's very nice."

Mama gasped, "Oh, no!"

"That woman has overstepped propriety." Papa was fully controlled now, but determined. "I'm going to talk to Gus and see if he can't do something about her."

Lillie spoke with anxious curiosity in every word. "Jerry, were you ever in Lucy's place?"

"Naw. Arnie won't let me deliver any groceries over there. Fact is, he's told me if I ever so much as sat on one of her benches in front of her place I'd never work for him again."

"Good for Arnie," Mama said with satisfaction.

I figured I'd better tell the whole story, because Mama or Papa would likely get it from Arnie anyway. So I told how Arnie got real upset and practically threw Lucy out of the place. When I finished Papa said, "The subject's closed," and he meant it, and it was.

The conversation wasn't too sprightly for the rest of the evening and Papa wasn't in the checker-playing mood, so I went to bed and read a couple of chapters from one of my Roy Blakely books before turning off the light and going to sleep.

The next thing I knew Papa was shaking my shoulder.

"Huh?" I mumbled.

"Come downstairs, Jer."

I skinned into my overalls and followed Papa to the front porch. Mama was there rocking away in her favorite chair. Papa sat down and so did I. We sat there in silence except for the squeaking chairs. It was a night to make you take notice, moonlight enough to give the lawn a mysteriousness, and fireflies almost looking like stars skimming around low and high. It looked to me as though they were having a convention. I'd never remembered seeing so many before. It was a funny thing. I couldn't be sure, but like I said, some were high and some were low, and I declare they were using those lights to talk to one another, for there was a rhythm about it and you would find one layer of them blinking on all at once. They would go out and another layer would come on. It was fearful pretty any way you looked at it.

There were a heap of noises, too. Ever since I was little we had had a pair of whippoorwills every year choose our place for their nesting. We figured it was the same ones all the time, and we'd given them names; Dusky, he was the boy, and Dilly, she was the girl. Well, anyway, Dusky was really going at it from a fencepost on the other side of Daisy's pasture. Now, a whippoorwill's song is bright enough and loud, but there's just something about it that makes a fellow moody-like, and while we were rocking away, I found myself being swayed by Dusky's music.

"Whip-poor-will! Whip-poor-will!" He carried on like he was trying to break an endurance record, and the longer he went, the sadder I got. Papa and Mama weren't saying anything, just rocking; Papa slow and easy, and Mama quick and nervous.

"Jerry," Papa finally said, and I could tell he was picking his words, "your mother and I feel it's about time to talk to you about, *hurrump,* certain things."

"Yes, Papa."

"Now, about Lucy."

"Yes, Papa."

Still slow and cautious he went on, "Southfield is a small town; a handful of homes, handful of people, yet,

99

Southfield is a cross section of the world. What goes on in Southfield goes on in the world. It has its share of nice people and its share of shoddy people, with a scattering of others in between. You've heard the worn-out saying, 'Birds of a feather flock together,' well, Lucy's place is a nesting hole for a flock of birds with dirty feathers.''

There was a pause and I said, ''An awful lot of people go there, Papa, and if you heap them all together, I reckon you'd have more'n half the men in town in a pile.''

''I know, I know, Jerry, and that's about par for the course.''

''It's a den of iniquity, that's what it is,'' Mama put in.

''You know what goes on there, Jerry?''

''Sure.'' I really didn't and was powerful curious and right off I knew I had answered too brassy.

''Hurrump,'' Papa cleared his throat.

''The men play pool there, and, and, and—''

Papa took it from there, ''And there's a great deal of drinking, although it's illegal. There's cards and dice, and, *hurrump,* other things.''

''It's a restaurant, Papa. Lucy's always sending over for supplies and she has as many as six waitresses working all the time.''

''Hurrump,'' Papa seemed disturbed. ''Exactly. Now let me conclude our discussion with a statement or two. Lucy and those who gather around her are people of bad reputation. They are guilty of practicing the evil the Bible condemns. Do you understand?''

''Yes, Papa,'' I said, which wasn't altogether truthful, because I couldn't remember where the Bible said anything about pool playing or card-playing or suchlike. I knew there wasn't any sense in carrying things on any further, but I thought I'd give it one more try. ''I figured if I worked over there I wouldn't let any of those things bother me.''

''Hurrump.''

It was Mama who put the clincher on it. She said softly, ''Jerry, we don't want you under any bad influences. We don't want your personality flavored by people who would gladly attempt to draw you into their filthy cycle of life."

There was something in Mama's tone that caught me off guard; something in her statement that wasn't out in plain view, and in a flash I knew it was the same thing that was in Papa.

Mama went on, while I tried to figure what this thing was that I couldn't put my finger on. "Lucy dirties everything she touches. Your father and I don't want you dirtied. We want you clean now and clean for the rest of your life. We want to be able to stand off to one side as the years go by and see our only son fine and upright."

Mama stopped and after maybe a minute Papa said, "Well spoken, Amy."

And there it was, that certain something that was there that I couldn't name. I right off knew it was there all along, but now it was out in the open plain as day, yet so secret you couldn't put it into words.

"I didn't want to work there much, anyway," I said offhand, feeling funny and choking up, and yet trying to act brassy. I was glad it was dark because, I might as well tell you, even though I kept swallowing and blinking my eyes there were tear pools forming and for the life of me I couldn't do a thing about them. It didn't help any when Mama's hand touched my left one, and it didn't help any more when Papa's hand came over and rested on my shoulder.

At first the chairs weren't rocking in rhythm, but being connected like that brought the rhythm about and away we rocked without saying much for maybe half an hour.

I almost made a big mistake. I almost told Mama and Papa about Mr. Strawman and John Kordick. I wanted to. The words were on my lips, but that plagued fear held me off.

Then I decided to, but at that moment Papa got up and said, "To bed we go," and I had lost my opportunity.

CHAPTER 8

HOEING A CORN PATCH can be comforting, especially when the earth is moist, the sun warm, and a body being barefoot like I was one morning about a week later.

Mr. Strawman and John Kordick had taken a back seat in my thinking and although Lillie's wedding day was taking about Mama's every waking minute, and Lillie herself was wilder than ever, things weren't bad.

I guess it was about eight o'clock when something else brought me a little more comfort. John Kordick passed by and spit in the general direction of our house, heading for Newark with his junky truck loaded high with crates of chickens.

On any day he went to Newark you could count on him being gone until late at night, so you can see how it was turning out to be an all-around promising day.

Maybe it was nine o'clock when Mama called, "Jerry, scoot up to Arnie's and get two pounds of stew meat."

Ever since Mr. Strawman's night I'd been ducking into the woods on the far side of the road when I passed Kordick's. Not today, though. Bold as brass I marched right by. I should say I started, but I didn't make it. I was looking at the house, thinking of what went on that night when Mousy Millie burst out on the porch.

"Jerry, you come here."

I stopped. I did more than stop, I froze. My feet were lead.

Mousy Millie called several times, but I was so startled I just stood there looking at her.

Across the porch, down the steps, down the stone walk, past the mailbox and across the street she came. What a sight! There were some old clothes in a trunk in our attic looking like the things she wore; clothes like you see in old pictures from when Grandma was a girl. A broadbrim hat, decorated with a flower garden, topped it off. Her dress was purplish with age, although once it had been black, and it dropped down clear to her ankles. Millie's running kicked up the dress enough to see she had black buttoned shoes on.

"I'm so glad you come!" Her skinny fingers grabbed my arms. "I need help." She tugged me toward the house. "I need help awful. Jerry, you hear me?" She shook me, "I need help."

I couldn't say a word. "We'd best get off this road so nobody can't see us." She kept tugging, but I stood as though I were planted in cement.

"I gotta go to the store for Mama," I blurted, finally finding my voice.

Mousy Millie's words tumbled out. "You go right along. Get what your Mama wants. Cart it on home. Then you come back to me. Oh, Jerry!" she wailed, "I need help awful bad. You just gotta help! I asked the good, dear Lord above to send along a body what I could trust. You come. Ain't that an answer to prayer? You hurry now, Jerry, and don't say nothin' to nobody. But you hustle back here," she whispered. "Don't worry none about Mr. Kordick. He ain't home."

She let go my arm and started for the house, going maybe six feet before she swung about. "You promise now, Jerry. You hear? You give me your word."

"Ma'am—"

She came back at me then, teary-eyed, trembly-voiced, bony hands wrestling with one another. "You promise! You gotta! The Lord above sent you."

"Ma'am, I could get into trouble." The teary moisture

in her eyes rounded out and spilled down her leathery face.

She came to me then and put her hands on my shoulders and pulled me down. "There ain't nobody else gonna help. You're the one the Lord sent."

While I was looking at her the skin on her face seemed to turn gray before my eyes.

I was a fool and what I should have said I didn't say, and what I should not have said I did say. "Yes, ma'am," and I pulled loose and ran toward Arnie's, never intending to keep my promise.

I waited on myself and got Mama's meat, cutting off all the fat and gitting rid of all the bone when Arnie wasn't looking.

I skirted Kordick's place and was considerably relieved to be in our house again.

Now that's a funny thing. Like I said, I had no intention of going back to Millie's—none. I left the kitchen and went to the barn. Before I knew it I was cutting through the woods straight for Kordick's place.

A promise is a promise and there I was stuck with it.

I wasn't bold or brassy going up to Kordick's. I was plumb scared. I hid in the bushes across from the house and there was Mousy Millie standing in the window, hands up under her chin, hat on, waiting.

I no more than had my head out in the open when Mousy Millie came flying out calling, "I knowed you'd come. I knowed you'd come."

I shuffled up the path, queasy-like, and was plenty jolted when I saw a brown paper bag lying in plain view at the bottom of the steps; wet and stomped on, but still a paper bag; one of the paper bags I had exploded on Mr. Strawman's night. I didn't have a chance to snag it. Mousy Millie was by my side, hauling and pulling me up the steps. It was night-marish, I will tell you.

Across the porch we went and through the door, with Millie spinning around and locking it the moment we were inside.

I had never been inside the house before and it was a

shocker to see. An empty barn with a milk stool and a bale of hay would have been better furnished.

It was clean enough, but naked, you might say. There was no rug on the floor and the wood was unpainted; whitish from many washings and uneven from lots of wear. One overstuffed chair faced the front window; the stuffing was pushing out of both arms and the seat. A straight-backed chair, with the legs held together by bale wire, leaned against the wall. An electric cord hung from the center of the ceiling with a socket and bulb attached to the end, and with a pull chain dangling down another six inches.

The dining room beyond was about the same; a walnut table with the varnish scrubbed away in five different places, leaving patches of light brown against the dark brown. Other than the table and two chairs there wasn't another lick of furniture in the room, except a light bulb hanging from the ceiling on a rope wire.

A rusty sink with a hand pump, a kitchen cabinet with white paint chipped and cracked, a coal stove set up on bricks and a rackety porcelain-topped table made up the furniture in the kitchen. There was no linoleum on the floor, no flowers on the windowsill, and it was about as depressing as living in a coffin.

Although I'd never thought much about it before, I realized Mama was a humdinger of a housekeeper; not over-neat, or anything, but homey. Every windowsill had some potted plant and Mama always had cut flowers, when they were handy, on all the tables. Besides that, she had enough pictures on the wall to keep a body interested for an hour looking at them. Rugs, too, ones she had made from discarded clothes, were everywhere, and when a new rug appeared I'd check to see how many of my old socks, pants or shirts were woven in with the other pieces of cloth.

Mama saved salt and pepper shakers, too, and they were tucked here, there and everywhere. They were a caution to dust but as bright and cheery as a rainbow.

Papa helped clutter up our house, too, as Mama often put it. From the time he was little he had taken a fancy to old

105

clocks and from time to time he would pick one up at an auction, bring it home, clean it up and either hang it on the wall, or set it in some handy place.

As far as furniture goes, we had it; not crowded, or overdone, but plenty, and a lot of it going back to olden times. I guess I never remember anyone coming to our house for the first time who didn't say how nice it was. And it was, too. It seemed nicer as I stood looking at Millie's.

"Mr. John Kordick a-cheated you, Jerry. He cheated you bad when you plucked them cherries fer him. Five dollars is what he cheated you from, that's what. Now come upstairs."

I didn't want to, but with the door locked I had no place to go so I followed Mousy Millie up a set of stairs that weren't comforting strong, but creaky.

Millie led the way to a room that ran clear across the front of the house. There was furniture here; musty ole stuff, but a heap of it. Off to one corner there was an oak desk: roll-top dozen-drawered, fifty-cubbyholed and almost as tall as I was. Two five-dollar bills were lying on top. Millie took one of them as though she were handling a robin's egg, and gave it to me. "It's your'n, Jerry. Tuck it in yer pocket."

I felt pretty good about this and was glad I came, after all. That feeling lasted about a minute. Millie took the other five-dollar bill and put it in my hand. "This is your'n, too."

"What for?"

"Because yer agoin' to help me, Jerry. I've took it about as long as I can. A body cain't live like this anymore. Mr. John Kordick is goin' plumb-bob outa his thinkin'. 'Twas always bad enough, livin' with him. My boys was good boys. They was dirt underfoot ter him. He drove 'em all away with his lickin', his hollerin', his threatenin', and his cussin'. I don't blame 'em none and every last one of 'em begged me to run off, too."

Millie took a couple sobs, so staggering big she bent over from the effort. "I couldn't do it, I couldn't run off, believin' it was a wife's bounden duty to stand by her wedded husband in thick or thin." Millie dabbed her eyes, "But it ain't been worth it. I hain't lived a decent day from my weddin' day on."

Millie sobbed a few more times and went on, with me wishing she would hurry up so I could get out of there. "It's worser now. Ever since that scarecrow come to plague him it's worser. Nights he don't sleep none, just sits here by the desk mumblin' names he figgered done it. I ain't never seen nobody so mindful to find out who tricked 'im. He'll do it, too. He'll find out. Then, like Arnie Beard said, they'll be a real murder in town, he's that determined."

"Millie, I have to go." My heart seemed like a chisel trying to carve its way out of my chest.

"Jerry, you promised."

"Well, tell me what you want me to do."

Millie didn't move. She dabbed her eyes. "Mr. John Kordick is drinkin' more. He drank some before, but mostly out in the barn and alone, too prideful to go to Lucy's more'n once a week. He don't care none no more. Walks right into Lucy's place every day."

Millie dropped her voice to a whisper. "He's treatin' other men. He ain't like that normal. He never bought nobody nothin' until now. I know why he's doin' it. He figgers people knows who tricked 'im and one of 'em will forget and slip out with the name. Then—" Millie's voice trailed off.

"I gotta go."

"Yer promised to help!"

"Help?" I said helplessly.

"Help me run off to Pittsburgh. I writ my boy, George, who lives there and says, 'Can I come ter live?' An' he writ back, 'We're waitin' fer you, Ma,' and I'm agoin', and yer gonna help me."

"Help?" I repeated helplessly again.

"Help me run off to Pittsburgh. I gotta get to the bus and get down to Newark to catch the train."

"You don't need help just catching a bus," I told her, easing toward the stairs.

"The bags is too heavy. One I couldn't carry, much less than two, loaded up the way them is an' all. You come on." She

107

started to pull me into a smaller room. "You can carry 'em."

There were two battered traveling bags on a bed; a bed that held a mattress and a blanket only.

"You mean you want me to carry those bags into town?" I almost choked on the words.

Millie looked shocked. "No, we gotta do it so nobody can't see us. We'll cut through the woods and come out on the road down below Arnett's farm at that lonely stretch. The bus'll stop fer me if I wave."

"Maybe there'll be somebody on the bus, maybe the driver, who'll tell. Most of those drivers know everybody in town."

Millie wavered. "I ain't thought of that, but I'm a-goin'." She brightened a bit, "And I know the good Lord is a-leadin'. They'll be a city driver on this bus and he won't know me. An' I'm a-countin' on the good Lord to have that bus empty of people, an' if there's people on it I'm a-countin' on the good Lord to have them keep their mouths shut. I'm a-countin' on the Lord an awful lot." She repeated it, "I'm a-countin' on the Lord an awful lot."

"If your husband ever found out I helped you, he'd likely kill me."

"The good Lord'll keep him from knowin', Jerry."

"Maybe if you took one at a time you could do it yourself," I suggested.

"Heft one of them bags, Jerry. You'll see I cain't do it myself."

She was right enough. I lifted the bag from the bed to the floor. It about buckled my knees, it was that heavy. It seemed like she had it packed with lead; pure, solid lead, at that.

"Why did you have to pick me?" I half wailed.

"Yer a good boy, Jerry. Most would tell on me. You won't. Yer a God-fearin' boy. I seen you goin' to Sunday school and church with yer little sister. Yer a good workin' boy. Arnie's said so many's the time. Like I told you afore, all mornin' I was a-prayin' the good Lord would send somebody by I could trust and yer the one that come. I needed help awful, and you come."

It wasn't often in my life I had anybody depend on me except maybe Betsy when I held her hand and led her across the road or gave her a glass of milk. Now here was a grown woman asking a favor.

"Please!" she cried, and I mean she actually cried with tears busting out again and those tears made me play the part of a fool. I grabbed the bags, felt my knees buckle but managed to stagger down the steps.

Millie's tears were working overtime when we reached the front door. "When a body's lived in a place thirty years 'tain't easy to leave." Millie unlocked the door, looked up and down the road, shed a few more tears, and said, "Hain't nothin' comin'."

The front porch creaked underneath me and the steps groaned as I descended. I didn't waste any time getting across the road and into the bushes.

We had about a mile to go but it was about the longest mile a body could imagine, considering how heavy and cumbersome those bags were. I'd walk a few feet, then rest, with Millie talking all the while. The more I heard, the more I feared John Kordick. It seemed to me he was more beast than man.

George, her oldest boy, endured Kordick's brutality until he was eighteen and then, not being able to stand it any longer, ran away from home. John, Jr., stood it until he was fifteen, and left. Horace skipped town when he was fourteen.

"I ain't seen one of my boys since they left. They never come back." It was a relief to finally plop those bags down behind a bush near the road.

"I better get on. I have to eat before I go to work."

Millie threw her arms around my neck and kissed me warmly and wetly. "Yer a good, good boy, Jerry. Just don't never say nothin'."

"Don't worry, ma'am, I won't. Good-bye now."

Millie paid me no heed. "I'm a-goin' to show you somethin'. Don't you never tell nobody." She knelt beside one of the bags and unfastened it. Right off I saw why they were so heavy. There were paper rolls, the kind you use for packing money and they were full; and there were loose coins, too; silver and gold ones, tucked in between the rolls. And there were packages of paper money. I'd never seen such a mess of money before and it is funny what that kind of a sight did to me.

"John Kordick never took a likin' to banks; never trusted them men who run 'em. Kept his money hid. He don't know I knowed where it was. I knowed, all right. But this hain't his money. It's money he stole from me. When my father died this money come to me from his will, but Mr. Kordick took it from me."

"How much is here?" My voice was as quavery as a screech owl's call; I was that astonished.

Millie lowered the lid. "Twenty thousand, to the penny. I hain't stealin' nothin', Jerry. I hain't happy doin' things this way, but the Lord knows I took more'n a body can tolerate. Now don't you never say nuthin' 'bout all this, Jerry."

"You'll never have to worry about that."

I left Millie standing behind a bush beside the road; gray, sad and yet somehow hopeful. I wasn't sorry I had helped her, but I wasn't glad, either.

It was a relief later to mount the two steps and pick my way through the merchandise Arnie had on display: a bag of red kidney beans and two bags of white beans with the burlap rolled neatly down, a box of plums, a keg of nails, a rack holding hoes and rakes, plus other things.

I let myself think for a moment perhaps the adventure of the morning was a bad dream, but it didn't work. A new fear had been born in me. It was different than the fear resulting from Mr. Strawman's work. Helping Millie was a serious thing and I knew it.

A car honked its horn in front of Clarence's gas station as I was about to push my way through the screen door. I whirled around and almost bolted for home, I was that frightened.

I got hold of myself and entered the store. It was downright pleasant to hear Arnie growl, "You're late!" This was normal. This was real. This was something I could handle.

"I'm ten minutes early."

"There's no room at the top for clock watchers." That was good to hear, although I had heard it hundreds of times before and hated it every other time. "Do you think the world owes you a living?" I'd heard that one, too.

"If you had your way," I countered sullenly, "I'd be here twenty-four hours a day and working every minute."

"Don't get fresh!" Arnie snapped. "I'm trying to help you."

"Well," I said, "Mama's going to talk to you about making me come early and keeping me so late every day."

Arnie's tone changed. "What's the matter with you, Jerry? You still look peaked."

That statement jolted me. That was something I didn't want to talk about so I ignored the question and hung on to the other subject. Something happened inside of me. I don't know whether it was anger, or just an explosion of emotions but I did something I never did to Arnie before. I shouted at him. "I work as hard as anybody in town. All you do is growl at me. I'd go over and work for Lucy in a minute if Mama and Papa would let me!"

"You told them about the offer?" Arnie asked mildly, lifting his straw hat with his thumb and forefinger and scratching the top of his head with the other three fingers.

"Yes, I did!" I snapped.

"And they said no?"

"They said no!" I still snapped.

"You got good parents, Jerry, good parents. Some would've thought only of the money, but not them, not them." His voice trailed off and he sat there scratching the top of his bald head for at least two minutes. "Of course, I can't pay you what Lucy offered," he finally said, "but you're a good boy. You work hard. You don't loaf." He paused again and a patch of sun slid between the Coca-Cola sign and the Campbell's Baked Bean sign pasted on the front window lighting up his bare feet perched on the rung of the stool. How swollen and pink his toes looked, like ten piglets lying asleep, side by side. "I'll give you twenty cents an hour and maybe we can increase the number of hours you work. How does that sound?''

It's hard to stay mad when a thing like that comes up. ''That sounds good to me,'' I said, mellow and friendly-like.

Arnie roared, ''Get to work! I'm not paying you to stand there gawkin' at me. You let that refrigerator go too long without cleaning. Clean it. And the mice around this place are getting fierce and bold as lions. Set traps.''

I went to work. When I got to thinking about it, I wish fear could be turned off like anger. A body can get angry sudden, and just as sudden it is gone. Fear might come sudden, and I guess some kind of fears could end sudden, but the kind of fear I had grew bigger and stronger.

It was a funny afternoon. I was pleasured because of the money, but my dread of Kordick's discovery of Millie's departure about buried my pleasure.

It was a busy afternoon. Customers flooded in and out and it seemed strange not to have them talking about Millie's running off. I found it hard to believe that I was the only one who knew about it and I half expected each new customer to blurt out the news. Mr. Wade came in, cheerful, friendly, smiling and gave Arnie a big order.

''Still feeding the men?'' Arnie asked.

''Tonight's the last,'' Mr. Wade said, ''and besides the workmen I have guests.''

''Hear you've made quite a few changes in the old mill.''

I was curious about the change in Arnie's attitude toward Mr. Wade. There was a change, all right. It was plain to see. I had noticed also that the last pamphlet was still on the cash register and it wasn't crumpled up.

''The men have done a good job. You'll have to come out and look the place over. Glad to have you spend an evening with me.''

The invitation caught Arnie off guard. ''I don't go out much. Store keeps me busy and my fee—'' He stopped, fumbling for words. It was the first time I had ever heard him slip up like that. I guess he knew it, too, and he finished lamely, "Come the end of the day I'm ready to sit."

When I got to thinking about it I realized that in all the years I had known Arnie I had never seen him out visiting anywhere, nor had I ever heard anybody invite him to their home or any place for that matter. It was a puzzle. People seemed to like him and even though he drove stiff bargains he was honest and people kept coming back. It was a mystery, all right.

For the first time one thing dawned on me; Arnie Beard likely talked to more people each day than any other person in town, yet he was lonely, and if Arnie was lonely, I figured his wife must be a heap lonelier staying home all day with no relatives to speak of, and never having had any children of her own.

Mr. Wade was talking. "I'd like to have you come, Arnie, and bring your wife."

I saw Arnie stiffen and he blushed, and that's something you don't see a man past sixty do very often. All at once I knew why. Mr. Wade had addressed him by his first name for the first time, and Arnie was pleased. "Well now, I might just do that—Julius."

After the order was filled and the bill paid, Mr. Wade, as he had done every time he had been in the store, took a pamphlet from his pocket and handed it to Arnie. "I think this is challenging, Arnie. Read it."

Arnie laughed, "You don't give up, do you?"

"No, sir, I don't"

"You might as well."

"Christ didn't give up on me and He won't on you." There was no discouragement in Mr. Wade's voice, but a quiet patience; a patience that seemed part of him.

"I'm an intellectual ridge runner." Arnie laughed. "When I was young I got tricked a couple of times into thinking a few people knew the answers to life. I ran after them for a while until I found out they didn't have any answers at all. Yes, sir, I've run a lot of philosophical, social, economic and religious ridges and at the end of each I tumbled off a cliff into a swamp; swamps, I tell you, that muddled my thinking, blurred my reasoning and finally dulled my trust in anything. Funny thing," Arnie mused reflectively, "every last one of them declared his philosophy was the only right one in the world, just as you likely think you're right. My mind's closed now to anything new."

You would think Mr. Wade would have been discouraged, but he wasn't. He said in that satisfying way of his, "I know what you mean, Arnie. While I never thought of it quite the way you do—running ridges and falling into swamps— I've taken a lot of mental excursions pursuing humanistic philosophies. I read a good many books in my time, listened to every intellect, real or assumed, that came to New York City. I never found any rainbows, either, so I gave up."

Arnie looked surprised. "Why plague me with yours, then?"

Mr. Wade chuckled easygoing-like and said, "That's it, Arnie. I gave up on the human attempt to answer the tough questions of life. I was driven to the divine answers and I found a rainbow of pure contentment, and as the years go by the colors in the rainbow grow more exquisite."

Arnie said reflectively, "A rainbow, huh? Seems to me the Bible hinted that the rainbow was only a promise." He tapped the ledger. "I've got a couple hundred names in this book with figures under their names showing how much they promised to pay. It's surprising sometimes to find out how hard it is to cash in on a promise."

"Not when the promise is Christ; not the historical Christ, though that's important; nor the Old Testament prophesied Christ, though that's important; not the symbolized Christ—I think the church has overdone that one; but the born, crucified, risen, coming Christ the Apostle Paul, led by the Spirit, makes so clear in his letters to the young churches."

Arnie shrugged, "A lot of the ridges I followed had the name Christ sprinkled all along the way."

"Get your eyes off the ridges then, Arnie, and look straight up and see Him as He is, rather than what man says He is."

I didn't exactly follow the conversation, but that's how it was. I helped Mr. Wade carry his order out to the car and when I returned Arnie was reading the pamphlet. He was interrupted three or four times by customers before he finished. He didn't crumple the paper up but laid it on the cash register with the other one.

"What's that one about?" I asked.

Arnie crooked his head around and read, "Four Witnesses You Can't Escape."

He lapsed into silence so I asked, making sure I was real busy so he wouldn't tell me to keep still and get to work, "What's it say?"

"It says that man is faced with four witnesses that would lead him to acknowledge God if he were honest," he said. Then he read,

1. Man could look at creation and come to the conclusion that God is behind it.

2. The fact that man has a conscience, the knowledge of right and wrong, would lead a man to acknowledge that God was behind it.

3. Man's logic, or ability to reason, in relationship to cause and effect, would lead a man to acknowledge that God was behind it.

4. If man would read the Bible it would lead him to acknowledge that God was behind it.

"In conclusion," Arnie was not as disturbed as usual, "it says if man doesn't accept these four witnesses and receive Christ as Saviour he is damned—doomed." Arnie snapped his fingers. "Lost." He turned on me viciously, "Now, do you understand what it says?"

"No," I said.

"Well then, spend your energy on your work and not on curiosity. Hard work, honest money are the two essentials for this life. When you can't produce the work and earn the money it will be time to die."

Actually it was sort of a fib to say I didn't understand it, for part of it I did. I believed there was a God. The thing that

115

puzzled me was He seemed so far off. Even when I went into church with the stained glass windows and the squeaky organ playing and Pastor Wallace using his preaching voice, God seemed out of reach to me. Yet, down deep I was as hungry for knowing the Lord as I was for a meal after going all day without one, and what with the clouds of fear hanging over me, I didn't want to have to face the future alone.

I was alone and I was terrified. I admit it. I kept thinking I was way too young to die and once or twice I got to feeling so sorry for myself I was brushing tears from my eyes, mourning over my own death.

While I was setting the mousetraps at five after six I tried to pray but I gave up after a couple of attempts.

CHAPTER 9

LATER ON IN THE EVENING I was putting Daisy out to pasture and Mama was working on her flower bed. Kordick drove by headed for home. It was a jarring finish to the day, and it was a restless night.

I decided to keep out of sight as much as possible so the next morning I finished my chores early, dug worms, found my cane pole, picked up a burlap bag to carry the fish I expected to catch and headed for the pond.

Although my mind didn't put it into words, I had a wee bit of hope I'd be able to talk to Mr. Wade.

Except for the meadow which extended from the mill to the pond's edge, the balance of the shoreline was pretty much overgrown with elderberry brush, willow and on the higher places, trees. It was an easy matter to keep out of sight and still do a lot of fishing. A filmy mist hung above the water at the south end of the pond and the surface of the water was mirror-smooth. Wind rippled the north end ever so gently. Patches of lily pads grew in the shallows. The mill, lovelier than can be put into words, appeared dreamlike through the mist. I don't know how a scene like that would affect others, but it did a funny thing to me. It made me ache, not in some part of my body, or anything like that, but I wanted to keep life just the way it was right then and there. It was so wonderful I never wanted to go back to town again.

I lollygagged around, as Joe would say, and finally fished. It wasn't long before I had two ten-inch bass and three sunfish. I put them in the bag and tossed it into the water so they'd keep alive and fresh. I baited up again and cast out and sat down.

The sun was just breaking above the trees when I heard a sound something like a horsefly making short trips with resting spells in between.

Someone else was fishing but I'd never heard anybody cast so often. Right off I figured it might be Joe McCormick. I was about ready to shout when I thought of Mr. Wade and not wanting him to hear me, I buttoned my lips just in time.

The horsefly sound came from my right and grew louder as the fisherman came closer. I hunkered over and spotted a pair of bare legs. A few more steps revealed a raggety pair of overalls, faded to gray-white, and a heap bigger than the person wearing them.

The brush stopped my view of the rest of the person. The elderberry brush was thicker off to my immediate right and the person disappeared behind it. I didn't bother concealing myself, still figuring it was Joe.

I was dead wrong for the person who stepped into full view wasn't Joe, nor was it a boy at all. No boy ever had long black hair braided down his back and tied with sprightly yellow ribbons at the tips. I wished it were a boy, for it's an uncomfortable feeling sitting in plain view with no chance to hide when there's a girl around who doesn't know you're there, and the way she was fishing showed she didn't know much. She used a long, skinny pole that wasn't much bigger around than a pencil at its thickest part. On top of that, she didn't let the bait settle at all, but kept it skimming across the top of the water.

When I got a look at the bait she was using it surprised me; her back cast brought it right above my head with a swish, and all it was was a bunch of feathers tied into an imitation of the most gaudy, unbelievable bug you've ever seen. No fish would ever bite a thing like that, I reckoned, and if it did, that pole she was using would bust for sure, as skinny as it was.

She was graceful, though, the way she did it, I have to admit. The line snaked back over her shoulder scattering drops as it came, then curled forward with the feather bug dropping on the water as light as a moth.

Suddenly the girl spotted my fishing pole. She swung about and gave a squeaky little gasp, "Oh! I didn't know anyone was here," not scared, just surprised. It confused me some, sitting there staring at a girl about my age, with eyes about as dark as wet charcoal, arms and legs about as brown as an Indian's, and so cool and undisturbed that she turned, reeled in her line and waded toward me.

For a crazy second she seemed like everything else around the pond that morning: soft, unnatural and, well— pretty—sorta.

It had been my custom to avoid girls as much as possible. Lillie was enough for me, and the ones in school were just smaller editions of her; talky, giggly, bossy, and all the time putting on that they're smarter than the fellows.

"Hello," she said.

Silly how a word like that could throw a fellow off as much as it did. I felt uncomfortably warm, although it wasn't that kind of a morning at all, and a pesky bunch of little prickly pins galloped up my backbone, heated up the back of my neck, crept around my cheeks, and had the top of my head tingling in no time.

I scrambled to my feet. "I was here first," I half-growled. Any way you look at it was a silly thing to say.

"Oh, I'm sorry!" She was, too. I could tell by the way she said it and the way she started to turn away from me.

"Oh, it's all right," I muttered. "Fish ain't bitin' any-way." Ain't is a word I seldom use, except when I want to act tough, and why I wanted to act tough then was a puzzle to me.

Anyway, she stopped and said, "Have you caught any?"

"Two big bass and three big sunfish."

"Oh, you've done better than I have." She sounded disappointed. "I only kept one so far."

"I know all the best places around here," I said. I felt superior. "Anyway, you ought to be glad you haven't hooked any big ones." I was glad to see I was a good five inches taller than she was and a heap bigger and heavier. "There are whoppers in here. If you ever snagged one of them that pole of yours would snap like a toothpick."

Her eyes seemed remarkably large and her skin was about as smooth—about as smooth—well, smoother than anything, and the sunlight glinting on her face with her smiling and all—well, it was confusing standing there, looking at her.

I walked over to my burlap bag and pulled it out of the water and opened it up. "Here's what I caught."

She laughed when she looked inside the bag; a soft, wavery laugh. "Would you like to see the one I caught?"

"Sure," I said in an offhand way. I started to follow her but stopped. "You'd better not walk out in the open that way. You'd better sneak through the bushes so you won't be seen."

She looked at me, smiling again, "Why?"

"Mr. Wade lives over there." I pointed toward the mill. "It's not likely he'd take to people fishing in his pond."

"You don't think he'd like me fishing here?"

"Nosiree!"

"Do you know Mr. Wade very well!" she asked, with that tantalizing smile fooling around her lips again.

"Well enough," I told her.

"Did you ask if you could fish here?"

"Look," I said, letting my voice go hard, "I've been fishing in this pond ever since I can remember. It was Mr. Kordick's then. He wasn't tolerant to trespassers, but I never asked his permission because he wouldn't have given it. It never stopped me, though." I whacked a pine branch with my hand. "Nobody's going to stop me from fishing where I want to."

"Perhaps Mr. Wade's different."

There was a bothersome tone in this girl's voice, not brassy or anything, but like she knew something I didn't know. "Not likely!" I snapped. "The kind of person who would have enough money to own all this land and fix up that mill the way it's fixed, ain't likely to give permission to a kid

120

like me. If I don't ask, he can't say no. So I come and go as I please."

"I should think you'd feel better if you'd ask Mr. Wade."

"Mr. Wade's a religious fanatic," I said, passing along Arnie's viewpoint. A trace of guilt tugged at me. "He's a reformer. He invades the privacy of a man's thinking."

The girl had been ahead of me when I said that. She stopped and turned around so quick I almost bumped into her. There was no smile on her face. "What?" she asked, cool and distant-like.

"Look," I said, "I work in Beard's General Store. What happens a couple of weeks ago? A stranger comes in and right off he slaps down a religious pamphlet. Next time it happens when he comes in, another religious pamphlet. Next time, another one. Arnie's plenty burned up about it, too, and so am I. Who's the stranger that does all that? Hah!" I snorted, "Mr. Wade."

The girl didn't move but stood about eight inches in front of me, away too close for my liking, but I wasn't going to back down. "It just may be," she said softly, "Mr. Wade wants others to believe as he does, so they have as much joy in life as he has."

"Ho?" I snorted. "Our town has enough crackpots already without another one." Down deep I knew I was making a mistake talking about Mr. Wade that way, but I plowed on. "This town doesn't need a religious reformer."

"What does it need?" How soft her voice sounded, and yet it wasn't soft, it was edgy. That girl was managing to get under my skin.

I raised my voice, "It doesn't need nothin'."

"When I came through it yesterday, it looked to me as though it needed a lot; ramshackled houses, peeling paint, rackety shingles, rutty roads."

"It's old," I said defensively. "It dates back to 1750."

"I took a good look at the people, too, sitting on those benches under the elm trees. If they'd get up and do some work—"

"They're retired," I countered

"They just looked tired to me."

You wouldn't think a girl who looked like that would be just like all the rest. "Well," I shot back, "it's good enough for me. Mr. Wade is wasting his time trying to reform Arnie. If he really wants to do something, let him tackle Fat Lucy, or John Kordick."

"Fat Lucy? John Kordick?"

"They're most uncommon sinners," I told her, "and any change Mr. Wade could work on them would be for the better."

She hadn't budged from where she'd been standing. The smile came back on her face. That smile was misleading. "How about you?" she asked.

"Me?"

"Don't you think you need some changing?"

"Nosiree! And if Mr. Wade knows what's good for him, he'd better not tackle me. I go to Sunday school regular and I stay for church off and on."

"You think that's enough?"

"It's enough for me."

Her smile broadened but it was the kind of a smile that said, "You're all wrong." If I could've thought of something to cut her down to size I would've done it right then and there. But I didn't have a chance.

She swung about and led the way to an open patch among the trees, kneeled down and lifted several handfuls of grass revealing the biggest bass I'd ever seen. I stared at it. I stared at her pole. I stared at her. "You didn't catch him with that pole."

"I caught four others, but I threw them back. They were only fourteen or fifteen inches long."

"You likely found him dead floating in the lily pads, or maybe somebody gave him to you." I knew she was telling the truth, but feeling as foolish as I felt made me stubborn. I would have said more but I heard Mr. Wade calling from the other side of the pond, "Rachel! Rachel!"

The girl stood up with her braids swaying ever so gently

as she turned toward the mill and called, "Coming, Uncle Julius!"

"You know Mr. Wade!" I blurted.

The same aggravating smile played around her lips. "I've known him all my life. My daddy is his agent and we're his guests."

She picked up the fish under the gills, not squeamish as most girls would be, but firm and sure, and headed around the edge of the pond. Before she passed out of sight she turned about and called, "Come back this evening, that's the best time for fishing with bass bugs. I'll prove to you this rod won't break." Back came that tantalizing smile, "And don't be sneaky about it, either. Come right up to the house and ask Uncle Julius for permission to fish with me."

I figured I had made about as big a fool of myself as a fellow could in the amount of time I had to prove it, so I said nothing. I went back to my burlap bag and dumped the fish in the pond. As they swam away I growled, "Go grow up, you runts!"

I walked home thinking about a lot of things, but most of all I was thinking about that girl, and it's funny how I couldn't get her out of my mind. It was pretty dumb saying, "Rachel," out loud like I did, seeing as how she was at the mill and I was a mile away.

It's funny, I didn't see the stump either, until I picked myself up after falling over it.

CHAPTER 10

I HAD NOTICED a change in Lillie as her wedding day approached; her voice reminded me of a sizzling firecracker, promising a coming explosion. I mentioned it to Mama and she told me it was a case of "premarital nervous jitters," whatever that is.

But Mama was worried. I overheard her tell Lillie, "You'll be so exhausted by the time you marry Roger your honeymoon will be a failure. Calm down, don't worry so much."

Lillie didn't, or couldn't, calm down and she kept on sizzling. I tried to keep out of her way and most of the time I managed it pretty well, but I made one big mistake.

I returned home after the fishing trip about eight-thirty, climbed the front porch steps, plopped into a rocking chair, hoisted my feet to the railing painted fresh white by Lillie the week before in preparation for the wedding, not noticing the trail of mud I spread behind me.

Lillie pushed the screen door open and stepped out. What a sight! She was wearing Papa's slippers, her own already packed for the wedding trip; one of Mama's old, discarded bathrobes, hers already packed for the wedding trip, and her hair was curled up in dozens of little rolls and tied with rags.

She walked to the railing on the far end of the porch, not seeing me. She stretched out her arms sort of toward the sun and breathed just loud enough for me to hear, "Ah, love! Sweet mystery of life!"

I didn't want to laugh, but I did. When she swung around I said, "If only Roger could see you now!"

"You!" It was a scream, a fury; the explosion had come. She saw the trail of mud. "You!" She headed for me, fingers outstretched like claws. I'm not sure what would have happened if she had caught me. I didn't wait to find out. I dove off the other end of the porch, stumbling forward into Mama's zinnia bed and breaking one plant, and headed for the barn.

There was a minute or so of remarkable silence, then came Mama's voice, cool and firm, "Jerry!"

I entered the kitchen and headed for the living room where I heard Lillie sobbing.

Mama met me in the doorway. "You get a pail of hot water, mop the front porch, steps, and the railing."

I turned and started toward the pantry to get the pail. Mama's voice, cool and firm, "And, she said, "when you've done that, mop up the kitchen."

When I looked at the floor there was no doubt about the need for it. My footprints were about as bold as Friday's were when Robinson Crusoe first saw them.

I finished up the two jobs and was putting the pail away when Lillie approached me. "Roger is due here in an hour." If Mama's voice was cool and firm, Lilly's was ice, and steel, "I'm not ashamed of my family; at least my mother, my father and my sister. But I'm very ashamed of my brother. He's a heathen; a thoughtless, self-centered, dirty, barefoot heathen. But I don't want Roger to know it. I'm making a request. Go comb your hair, why you let it grow so long in the first place I'll never know. Go put a clean shirt and clean pants on and—" she measured her words, "you've washed your feet to your ankles, wash them to your knees, put socks and shoes on."

Now that's the kind of lecture I dislike and I was about to tell Lillie so, along with a few other things, when Mama appeared. All she said was, "Thank you, Jerry," cool, firm—but it was a warning with a begging tied into it, so I gave in.

125

I was coming downstairs about fifteen minutes later when Roger pulled into the driveway. I knew it was Roger, for he always honked his horn in tune with "Shave and a haircut, two bits."

Lillie fled, rag curlers flopping, Papa's slippers scuffing, Mama's bathrobe flaring.

I went out the back door and Roger was unloading some of the filthiest lanterns you ever saw from his car. "Hi, Jer! I'll give you a dollar for helping me clean up these things."

"Sure," I replied and helped carry them into the barn where I had the others lined up. We set to work cleaning them up at Papa's workbench.

I was polishing the brass bottom of my first lantern when I asked Roger, "How come you want to get married?" figuring on maybe warning him again.

"A good question, Jerry, but a fellow needs a girl."

"I don't!" I snapped.

"Yet," Roger said, "but you wait. You wait. You'll be rolling along like I was, then you'll see her. Her eyes will be bluer than the sky, or maybe darker than black-eyed susans. She'll have the cutest nose, the blackest, the brownest, or the blondest hair you've ever seen. Everything she says will be delightful and—" he took his left hand off the lantern he was cleaning and snapped his fingers, "that's it!"

"Never!"

"Wait."

We worked for a little while and a nibbling plan wormed its way into my mind. I said, "It's awful hot. It'd sure be a relief to kick a fellow's shoes and socks off, wouldn't it?"

"When I was your age I kicked 'em off when school let out and left them off until school started in the fall, except for special occasions."

I said it innocent-like, but the keen edges of my thoughts were carving out a plan. "Nobody's to stop us from enjoying ourselves. Let's take ours off."

It was that simple. In a minute we were barefoot.

"Look, Roger, Lillie's going to be out in a couple of

minutes. Then you won't even know I'm around. How about looking at the biggest squash I've ever raised?''

Roger didn't hesitate but followed me out of the back of the barn to the garden patch. No one could have walked between the rows of tomatoes, corn, cucumbers, and finally the squash vines without getting some dirt on his feet, unless he was very careful. Roger wasn't at all careful; fact is, while we were admiring the squash he bored a hole in the soft cool dirt with his toes until his foot was clean buried—I mean dirt buried—to his ankle.

We returned to the barn. Maybe twenty minutes passed when I heard the screen door on our back porch open and shut; not noisy as usual, but gentle. I knew it was Lillie.

"I'll be back in a minute," I said to Roger, and headed for the house, planning to let Lillie see me before she saw Roger.

Lillie was a picture of sheer expectant happiness: bright yellow dress, stockings, good shoes, hair done just so. She saw me, stopped and gawked, then sizzle-whispered, "You! I begged you! You march up—"

Her voice drained off. She looked beyond me toward the barn. "Roger!" She didn't whisper the word, but it was as soft and gentle as a whisper.

Roger came toward her, pants rolled to the knees, both feet muddy. He kissed her, not caring that I was right there watching, and led her to the barn; Lillie not so much as even mentioning his bare feet. I didn't bother following, but loafed around, feeling satisfied and cagey, too.

Lillie came out of the barn while I was loafing on the back steps. I figured she would crawl all over me, but, nosiree! That girl never noticed me. It was as though she were sleepwalking; went right by me, never so much as glanced my way.

Five minutes later she came out again. It wasn't the same Lillie that went in. No yellow dress, but wearing the very shirt and jeans I had worn fishing that morning; dirt and all. And, believe it or not, as barefoot as the day she was born. It shook a body to see a thing like that.

I walked down to the brook, rinsed off my feet, went to the front porch and settled in a rocking chair. It's been said that sitting down and going over a body's problems will help solve them. I went over my problems all right, the Lillie problem, the Kordick problem, and that Rachel girl problem. I'd show her, I figured.

I guess I sank into sleep because I was dreaming of hauling in a monstrous big bass with her looking on, when Mama shook me. "Jerry, have you forgotten it's Saturday? You're due at Arnie's at one. It's twelve now. Lunch is ready."

I figured the first thing I would hear from Arnie was that Millie was missing, but nosiree! Nor did I hear it from anyone that day, which was a relief and I figured maybe she had given up the idea of running off and managed to get back home with those bags.

After supper I headed for the pond to meet that Rachel girl. The closer I got, the less brassy I felt and I ended up by sneaking through the brush and looking for her from a hiding place.

I saw her all right, but she sure wasn't ready to go fishing, I didn't think. She was on the porch, wearing a white dress, and her hair was all loose and tumbling down her back in waves.

Mr. Wade was there, too, with another man; that Rachel girl's father, I figured. It was very plain to see, the way she was dressed, and all, there was no point in marching up and saying, "Are you ready to go fishing?" I returned home and I don't know how I felt, but it wasn't good.

Papa had come home, so the evening wasn't a total waste.

I was some surprised the next day to see that Rachel girl, her father and Mr. Wade in church. I went about my way without letting on I saw her, but she saw me, I knew that. I felt her eyes on me more than once. But after what she did the night before I made up my mind to ignore her.

I managed to get right behind them when the service was

128

over and I was close enough to hear Mr. Wade say to Pastor Wallace, "A most refreshing message, sir. I'm pleased to find a Bible-believing church in town."

That surprised me, for I wasn't refreshed. If it hadn't been for the fly I caught and played with, I'd likely have gone to sleep.

Time is funny stuff. A body can't see it. He can't stop it. He can't start it. He can't hold on to it and he can't let it go. It's about the most independent stuff there is. Sometimes it works against you, sometimes it works for you.

It worked for me. By that I mean the more of it that passed the less I worried about Mr. Strawman and Mousy Millie and getting back at that Rachel girl.

The weather too made a fellow lazy-acting and lazy-thinking. A hot spell set in; settled down, you might say, for a long stay. Folks that had a chance sat a lot, talking low, not moving much, sweating plenty. Lucy's benches were jammed full and most of the men had a roll of newspaper in their hands. After they had read it, it came in handy for a fan or a flyswatter.

The flies were about the liveliest things around and plentiful. Arnie was death on them. It was my job now every afternoon to take the swatter and rid the store of them, and after each death blow to pick them up by lifeless wings and drop them into a paper bag, for if there was one thing Arnie hated more than live flies around the store, it was a dead one, especially in the display cases or in the windows.

So life was easy once again, and lazy, for twice John Kordick came in, the Kordick of old: not raging, not talking about anything much except the weather, but moist from sweat and sour-faced, and with a matchstick rolling about in his mouth.

There was no sign of Millie, and Arnie asked about her. "Millie?" Kordick said easily, "Heat's got her beat." And that was all.

But she was gone, I knew, for though Arnie didn't notice it, Kordick was buying only enough for one to eat. I got to thinking it was to his pleasure she was gone and now maybe I had done him a favor in helping her, but either way the situation wasn't so worrisome.

On Thursday afternoon Miss Perry came into the store. It was surprising how much she could brighten up a place. Like I said before, there wasn't another soul who could, just by walking in, stir up so much enthusiasm, happiness, or whatever it was she had. It came in with her now.

"I've got news, Arnie!" she announced, opening up her purse at the same time and pulling out a clipping from a newspaper.

Then Gus, I mean our chief of police, (only where Miss Perry was concerned he never acted like the chief of police, but like a country yokel of maybe seventeen) came through the door, and as usual, he acted, or tried to act, surprised at seeing her.

"Oh, hello! Have you decided about tonight yet?"

"The answer's still no," Miss Perry said, which was an odd answer if you didn't figure Gus had probably been pestering her half a dozen times that day by phone calls, or maybe pulling up in front of her house in the police car.

"This isn't gonna be any ordinary auction. There will be real bargains; pots and pans, dishes, and I heard tell there's a whole houseful of furniture as good as new."

This talk would have been surprising, too, unless you knew Gus had been pestering Miss Perry to get married ever since before she went away to college.

"Gus, I'm washing my hair tonight. I told you that."

"It looks all right to me."

It did to me, too; dark, long and glossy as it was.

Miss Perry said to Arnie, trying to ignore Gus, "Do you know anything about that new man in town?"

"You mean Julius Wade?"

"Professor Julius Wade," Miss Perry said with emphasis. "He's been a professor at Columbia University for thirty years. He's retired now. This clipping from the *New York Times* tells about his moving here. Not only that, do you know something else?" She hurried on without waiting for an answer, "The history books our school has been using for the sixth, seventh and eighth grades were written by him. And not only that, he's at work now on a new book."

"Let me see that," Arnie said. He took the clipping, read it, handed it back and said, "Well, you never know. You never know."

"Think of that! A famous historian right here in our town!"

"Well, you never know," Arnie repeated as though he hadn't heard Miss Perry's last statement, but just sort of stared out the window at the old elm trees with their leaves hanging hot, motionless, almost lifeless in the scorching sun.

"Look," Gus butted in, "couldn't you wash your hair tomorrow night?"

"Oh, all right, Gus," Miss Perry said without so much as looking in his direction. "Now let me talk to Arnie for a minute."

Gus went out of the store happy and victorious. "Be ready at seven," he said, holding the screen door open long enough for a number of flies to come through.

"I was thinking, Arnie, you're a member of the school board. Wouldn't it be a good idea to invite Mr. Wade to speak to the PTA?"

"I s'pose, I s'pose," Arnie answered without anything in his tone except puzzlement.

That news was a puzzlement to me, too, and I wondered how an intelligent man like Mr. Wade could believe in things he couldn't see, if the whole idea were as questionable as Arnie claimed it was.

Miss Perry left the store and with her went a shaft of sunlight on a garden of roses. That may sound a little far-fetched, but I'll tell you something, it wasn't far from the truth.

The whole thing left Arnie touchy. He sent me to the back of the store to wash down the shelves while he sat on the stool, bare feet resting on the lower rung, hat pushed back, pencil stuck in the brim, cheeks red and, generally speaking, a picture of gloom.

The atmosphere wasn't helped any when Kordick shuffled in about twenty minutes later. Miss Perry's brightness made Kordick's darkness darker; dirty matchstick hanging from his moist lips, dirty-shirted, unshaven, sweaty, and although I was in the back of the store his personal smell hit me: a mixture of barn, pigpen and clothes worn too long.

"What do you want, John?"

Kordick worked the matchstick across his lips, not saying anything, but glaring at Arnie.

"I told you not to come in here if you'd been drinking, John."

"Ya know, don't ya, Arnie?"

"Know what?" Arnie snapped.

"About Millie."

"Millie? What do I know about Millie?"

"You know she's run off."

"Didn't know it, but don't blame her."

Kordick leaned over the counter and pushed his face to about eight inches from Arnie's, but Arnie didn't back away. Kordick didn't say anything right off and it was like waiting for a dynamite blast to explode, there was that much tension. "Ya do know, don't ya?" he finally said. His voice was so slurred he sounded almost like an animal and just as dangerous.

Arnie stiffened. "I'm not sure I follow you," he said, in a different tone, almost as though talking to a child. "Tell me what you're talking about."

The tension broke and Kordick pulled away, and while his words were slurred there was a change; a hopelessness in him. "Millie's run off. Last Friday I come back from Newark; house empty, Millie gone. No food cooked. Figured she'd come back. Didn't say nothing. She didn't. Got to thinking." He paused and looked out the windows toward the street. His voice dropped lower. "Got to thinkin' and I looked, and it was gone. It was gone. She took it, but she had to have help. She couldn't 't heft all that without help. Found out this morning. Gone, I tell you, gone! Her and it—gone! But somebody helped her tote it."

"John," Arnie interrupted softly, "what are you talking about?"

"It'd take a man to heft that. Too heavy for Millie, so she's run off with a man, and she's cleaned me out."

"Money?" Arnie questioned.

"Over seventy-five thousand dollars."

"What!"

"First off I figured she'd come crawling back beggin' and I wouldn't of took her." He rambled on, grotesque, sickening, saying all kind of things and using words I can't use—bad words and it was fearful to hear him talk.

"Never knowed she knew where I kept it, and her planning all the time to run off with somebody. Sneak! Likely she was in on that other thing. Lookin' back at it now I figger she knowed who set up that scarecrow. Likely helped 'em. Woman never was worth nothin'. Couldn't work a lick. Spoiled them boys, babyin' them. Made them lazy louts."

John stopped and spit on the floor and that spit was like poison from a rattlesnake it was that disagreeable.

Arnie stood up. "Kordick, I put you out of this store once and now I'm doin' it again, and this time it's permanent. If you ever step in this place again I'll have Gus arrest you for trespassing."

Kordick repeated, "Gus!" then added some awful words and he spit again.

"Get out!" Arnie was around the counter. "Get—out!" he shouted. "I don't blame Millie for going off, and if she took the money she had it coming. You've never done a thing for her. You ruined her. I remember when she was a beautiful girl. You've been chokin' the life out of her ever since. And I knew your boys. There weren't three brighter boys in town, nor harder workers." Arnie couldn't contain himself. He shouted at the top of his voice, "Get out of here!"

Kordick spit again at Arnie's feet but it didn't stop Arnie, and Kordick turned and went for the door.

I figured Arnie would call me to clean up the mess Kordick had made and I don't think I could have done it, but he didn't. He did it himself and I guess he scrubbed those three places no less than ten times each and with scalding hot water, a scrubbing brush and the strongest soap we had in the store. When he finished he went back to his stool and he looked downright sick, and tuckered out, and you can guess how I felt.

CHAPTER 11

SLEEP WAS HARD to come by that night what with my mind filled with more thoughts than I could handle. Mama and Lillie worked on the wedding dress and they came upstairs around twelve, talking softly. I heard them get into their beds, heard the motion of their bodies as they got comfortable, and then after a time their heavy breathing as they slept.

I suppose it was 'most two o'clock by the time I dozed, but not for long. Something woke me, or at least roused me to semi-consciousness. Downstairs I could hear the ticking of the clock and from my open window I heard the pigs stir. And the wind was there, moving through the maples, oaks and pines. All this was normal, but there was something abnormal and it was almost no sound at all.

Above the other noises, or maybe I ought to say beneath them, there was a fuzziness, a fuzziness like the sound of two rough pieces of cloth rubbing together. It was different, but not frightening, for Rusty was silent, and if there was anything I ought to know Rusty was trustworthy. He would have been barking. But he wasn't, so I lay there.

The sound became a presence, something was outside and when it ceased to make any noise at all it was still there.

I studied the window and framed it out in my vision by the blackness of the room and the deep blue-blackness of the sky above. I thought of a heap of things in those few minutes: moth wings against the screen, Rusty scratching a flea, Daisy rubbing her side against the pasture fence. Now a thing like that can be a bother and I got to thinking that to find out what it was was the most important thing in the world. I was listening so hard it set me rigid and I got to sweating.

A creak; so soft it was hardly a sound at all. Rubbing again, even softer, and that presence was there.

I stared at the window so intently that the black and blue-black merged together and I had to blink to get it back into view.

I eased my way across the bed and sank to the floor; looking upward, I caught a couple of stars.

Another creak: sharp, distinct—on the porch roof, near my window.

A star disappeared, then another.

A silhouette filled the window.

One thing—one thing only—filled my mind. Kordick! He had come. He had found out!

I could hear him breathing; hear his fingertips rub across the screen and his fingernails prying at the wooden frame. While I stared the stars were there again, the frame was empty.

I wanted to laugh. I wanted to shout, my relief was that great—a dream.

I stood up and was about to get into bed when the sounds were there again. I sank to the floor. No stars.

I moved backwards toward the door, reached up and felt on the shelf where I kept my rock collection. With lodestar accuracy my right hand slid around a chunk of quartzite.

I heard the screen frame squeak, pried loose now.

Away, way off some place, away way off a dog barked, not Rusty. In my misery my heart ached because of his betrayal.

I stood up. I screamed. I hurled the rock.

It smashed the double panes of glass above the shadowy figure. Glass cascaded down. A snort, sucked breath, rustling, all this came from the roof: a crackling, a thump, explosive breath, and the sound of running. And Rusty did not bark.

Mama was at my doorway. The light came on.

"Jerry! Why, Jerry! Whatever have you done?"

"Someone—" I almost said John Kordick, "someone was trying to get through my window."

"Jerry, son, you've been dreaming. You're as pale as a sheet."

"No dream," I could barely talk, my chest ached that much, and my breath seemed all but choked off.

Lillie came in yawning. "What's the matter, little boy? Did you fall out of bed?"

Betsy's voice came down the hall, half crying, terrified, "Mama?" She came into my room, came into Mama's arms all in one movement.

"Rusty didn't bark."

Lillie was composed and not alarmed at all. "Why should he bark at your imagination?"

"He killed Rusty, that's why." I guess I was crying. Anger, fear and sad relief at the possibility of Rusty not being a betrayer after all.

"Nonsense!" Lillie said, turned, switched on the hall light and went downstairs brassy and bold. I heard her at the kitchen door. "Here Rusty! Here Rusty!"

Mama talked. "Jerry, it was just a dream. Why would anybody want to break into our house?"

"I dunno," I mumbled, "but someone was there—I think." My words were limp, "I know it."

Downstairs Lillie was still going at it, "Here Rusty!"

"Rusty would have barked," Mama said.

"Rusty's dead," I blurted. "Lillie's been calling. He hasn't come."

Lillie's tone changed, "Ah, good boy! Where were you, chasing a rabbit?" and calling, "He's here!" and they came up the stairs, Rusty running into my room first, wagging his tail, excited, panting and sniffing at the window.

Lillie followed, "I told you something's wrong with Jerry, Mama. He's been acting real odd lately. Sort of like he's guilty or has a secret he doesn't want anybody to know about."

Mama said wearily, "I can't scold you for having a dream, Jerry, but this is going a little too far."

137

"I'm going to bed," Lillie announced.

Mama and Betsy left with Lillie, but Lillie was back in a second or so closing my door. "No use letting mosquitoes take over the whole house. You'd better turn your light out. You'll be eaten alive as it is." She closed the door none too gently.

I turned off the light and sat on the bed. Rusty came over and tried to nuzzle me, but I shoved him away hard. He came back and tried again. I was that fed up with him I took him downstairs and put him out.

Lillie was right about the mosquitoes and within half an hour I was out of my room, downstairs on the couch, but it didn't help my sleep any. I tossed and turned until dawn.

Mama came downstairs early. She sat on the couch beside me. "Jerry," she whispered.

"I'm not asleep, Mama."

"I didn't think so. Lillie has me thinking, Jerry. You have been acting strange lately. Is there something you'd like to tell me?"

"No, Mama," which was another one of my big lies. Then I burst out, not even thinking, but bitter, "Papa ought to be here! Having him is like having no father at all. Him being away all the time. What's he do, come home a handful of hours a week. If he really loved us, would he go off like that?"

"He's a salesman, Jerry!"

"Salesman! Salesman! He'd change jobs if he really loved us, really."

Mama answered, not defensively, but sternly loyal, "Papa does the best he can. If you knew how hard he works and how hard he tries to get home you'd know how much he loves us."

"He should have a job near home," I insisted.

"He's tried, Jerry, but times aren't easy."

"Well, if he loved us he'd try harder."

"You're unfair, Jerry."

I knew it, but I wasn't going to admit it. "I'm not! He could if he set his mind to it." I'd never talked to Mama that way before. I knew it and Mama knew it, and Mama knew that I knew it, and I couldn't have hurt her more if I'd tried. She sat there saying nothing with dawn's light showing me the tears in her eyes. She didn't cry, but bit her lip and looked forlorn, and that's the way she stayed for maybe ten minutes.

Lillie broke the spell. She hollered from upstairs, "Mama! Jerry!" like there was somebody grabbing her hair.

Mama was on her feet first, but I was past her before she got to the stairs. Lillie was geared high. She grabbed my arm when I reached the hall. "You were right, Jerry! There was somebody on that roof last night."

I headed toward my room and I'll say one thing, I sure had done a job with those windows. There were a few broken pieces on the floor and a mass of glass scattered all over the roof. There was something else too: blood, lots of it, blackish red against the brown shingles.

Some spots were the size of dimes and some the size of your hand.

There was something else there, too, a whip, an old-fashioned buggy whip, long, and black, with a tassel of thick leather strands dangling from the end.

Mama was sober and she took me by the arm firmly. "Jerry, do you have any idea who it was who would be trying to get into your room with a thing like that?"

"No, Mama."

"Have you been in a scrap with any of the boys?"

"No, Mama."

"Jerry," there were tears in her eyes, "this is serious. Isn't there anything you can tell me to help?"

"No, Mama."

Mama's questions were a problem, but I'll tell you, Lillie was a problem, too. She stood there studying me so hard I figured she was trying to read my mind and maybe being successful, because my mind was working overtime.

As soon as I could get away I went outside where Rusty met me. He jumped, he barked, he wagged his tail, he hunkered his head down between his front paws, he whined,

139

he did everything he knew how, to get me to pay attention to him, but I was so disgusted I only growled, "Get out of here, you tramp!" but he wouldn't go.

When I found a trail of blood leading from the back porch to behind the barn, Rusty was ahead of me, sniffing and leading me until we got to the old apple orchard. I found a place there in the deep grass where it was all pressed down and there was more blood. And there was a handkerchief soaked with it. I tried to follow the trail from there but couldn't, and Rusty lost interest and wasn't any help at all.

I didn't tell Mama or Lillie about this discovery, nor did I tell Gus, for he came in while we were eating breakfast. Mama had called him as soon as I had left the house. I'll tell you something; if Mama's questions were gritty, and if Lillie's looks were gritty, that Gus was a terror. He ate breakfast with us and I guess there wasn't a minute when he wasn't poking a question at me and I kept answering about the same way I did Mama.

"It's not normal," he said shaking his head. "It's just not normal. No intelligent person would climb on that roof with a whip. So, he was either a fool by nature, or a fool by drinking, or a fool by anger. Can you help me out, Jerry. Which one would he be?"

"I don't know."

"There's one more possibility and this is the one I hold to, Jerry, you've had a hassle with one of the boys, haven't you?"

"No, sir."

"Maybe you just don't remember," he said sarcastically.

I figured it was a good place to stick in another fib. "Well, maybe."

Gus jumped on that. "That's more like it. Do you want to tell us who it is and why he wanted to get back at you?"

"No sir," I mumbled, encouraging belief in my lie.

"If I'm any judge, that boy will be easy to spot, for no one could bleed that much unless he was cut up considerably."

He said reassuringly to Mama, "Amy, boys' mischief. Don't be too concerned."

All morning I kept wondering why Rusty hadn't barked. Along about eleven-thirty a thought hit me that about laid me flat. The only person, outside of our family, who could approach our house without getting barked at was Joe McCormick. Rusty was used to his coming over 'most any time, day or night. But what would Joe be doing with a buggy whip, and he always stayed near the barn and whippoorwill-whistled.

It was a puzzler, so I decided to walk over to Joe's and find out. He wasn't in the barn, nor in the fields, so I stood by the back porch and whistled as I usually did.

Mrs. McCormick came out. "Looking for Joe, Jerry?"

"Yes, ma'am."

"He came downstairs this morning looking poorly, so I marched him up to bed again," she told me.

"Thank you, ma'am," I said, standing there waiting to ask more questions but Mrs. McCormick went back into the kitchen.

Why would Joe be pulling something like that? I'll tell you something, it's not a nice thing to know your best friend doublecrossed you, and I figured on fixing him. Yet, the more I thought about it, the more unreasonable my suspicions seemed.

Work in the store that afternoon was not easy. News of Millie's running off was common knowledge and John Kordick, from what I gathered, had consumed enough whiskey at Lucy's place to set him talking, and talk he did, claiming that some man helped her.

Fat Lucy came over from her place, brazen, brassy and enjoying the whole thing and said, "Millie wasn't worth much and the man who ran off with her didn't get much, but the hundred and fifty thousand he got made the whole thing worthwhile."

"Seventy-five thousand," Arnie corrected wearily.

"Seventy-five thousand, hundred and fifty thousand," Lucy laughed, "both's the same to me. I know a heap of men

141

who'd be glad to have Millie for that price. How about that, Jerry Berry? You'd help Millie run off if you could get that much, now wouldn't you?''

How is a fellow going to answer a question like that?

Arnie snapped, ''Woman, stop!''

Lucy came close and fawned over me, smelling of strong perfume and powder, and patting my cheek. ''You're pale, Jerry Berry.''

''I'm aw-right,'' I mumbled, trying to back off.

Lucy turned away, ''Shouldn't take much doin' to find out who run off with her. John's found something; a clue you might say. Claims as soon as he finds out who owns the thing he found he'll have the culprit.''

''What'd he find?'' Arnie asked.

''I didn't ask, not being the curious type,'' she rambled on, and she looked at me again, ''Jerry Berry, you better return that hundred and fifty thousand—and Millie.'' She was laughing, but I wasn't. ''John wouldn't like a tad like you pulling a trick like that.'' She dropped her voice to a whisper. ''Jerry Berry, tell me where you got her hid.'' She gave a loud, brassy laugh, and left the store with her arms full of groceries.

I'll tell you this, she wasn't any comfort to a soul.

The following Monday was a scorcher; so hot about every living thing—pigs, chickens, Daisy, Rusty (whom I hadn't forgiven), and the birds—were all quiet and holding tight to the shade. I did, too, and was loafing out of the sun beside the barn. I hadn't seen Joe. The two times I went to his house his mother said he was still poorly, and he hadn't shown up for Sunday school the day before. I was convinced he was the one on the roof that night and was making out he was sick, just to avoid me. But I couldn't figure out why he would do a thing like that.

I was thinking about it when who walks around the side of the barn but Joe himself, sorta palish, but without a scratch on his face or hands.

''I thought you'd be cut up,'' I growled.

''What do you mean, cut up?''

"You know, wise guy."

"Know what?"

The way he said it convinced me he didn't know what I was talking about so I told the whole story.

"How come you thought it was me? Why would I do a thing like that?" he asked with hurt tones.

"Rusty didn't bark, and you're the only one that could come around here without him letting me know."

"Well it's a snap somebody else has made friends with him, because I sure wouldn't do a thing like that—hey," he said, changing the subject, "it's this Saturday Lillie gets married, isn't it?"

"Yup, and just wait until that Roger finds out he's marrying a wildcat."

"It's sure going to be a wingdinger of a wedding, huh?"

"I reckon."

We chewed the fat for a while and Joe left, leaving me more confused than ever. I rethought the thing and figured it must have been Kordick who had been on the roof after all. Rusty came up and licked my hand and I clouted him a good one, I was that upset.

I had to go to work that afternoon at twelve to make up for missing the coming Thursday and Friday when Mama wanted me around the house to help in preparation for the wedding. Papa was planning to take off those two days so he could help, too.

CHAPTER 12

IT'S A FUNNY THING how quick old news items are replaced by new ones. I didn't hear much about Millie, or Kordick that afternoon, but I did hear a lot about the wedding. Fact is, the afternoon turned out to be really pleasant, though hot.

Mr. Wade walked in and that Rachel girl was with him. I'll tell you, she was a sight. She had on a yellow dress. Her hair wasn't hanging down in braids, but was pulled back and tied at her neck with a yellow ribbon. Altogether she looked cooler than the inside of our icebox. As soon as she saw me she pounced.

"What happened? Were you afraid to come back that night?"

"Nope."

"I just guess you were."

"Nope."

"Why didn't you then?"

"I did, but you weren't decked out for going fishing. I saw you all dressed up, sitting on the porch."

"So you were there! Were you afraid to march up like I told you to and ask Uncle Julius for permission?"

"Naw, just wasn't interested in messin' around without going fishin'."

"I planned to change," she said. "I could've been ready in a jiff."

Mr. Wade chipped in, "I hear you claim my pond is your pond, young fellow."

"Fished there all my life," I said defensively.

Mr. Wade laughed, "Well, let's say you own the fishing rights, then."

"Come tonight," Rachel said, "unless you're afraid."

"I'll be there."

As usual Mr. Wade left a pamphlet and Arnie took it without mumbling at all.

It's a funny thing how the afternoon changed after they were there. The heat didn't seem to bother me nearly as much, and that Rachel girl somehow reminded me of Miss Perry. I mean, when she came in, well, it was different, that's all. Somehow brighter and cheerier, but I couldn't put my finger on just why.

I ducked out at six, ran home sweating plenty, whipped through my barn chores, grabbed a bite to eat and headed for Wade's place.

That Rachel girl was there, still wearing the yellow dress, but without her shoes and socks. She had already been fishing and announced, "I guess the heat's driven them to deep water where it's cool."

"You can be glad," I shot back, " 'cause like I said the other day, that pole of yours would go to pieces if you caught one more than two or three inches long."

"You saw the one I caught."

"Found dead of old age."

"I'll show you."

But she didn't, and I didn't catch anything either, and after a while we quit and sat down on a fallen tree, dangling our feet in the water, watching the sunset.

Our conversation went along first rate, with her telling me about living in New York and how she'd traveled all over the West and even to France. Her father was a writer's agent; he's the one who took care of Mr. Wade's books. Everything went along first rate, that is, until I said, "It's hard to see how a smart man like Mr. Wade would get tangled up in religion."

"It's brilliant men like Uncle Julius who are curious about life. They want to know the answers."

"Answers to what?"

"Where did I come from? What is my purpose in life? Where am I going?"

"Aw, who knows the answers to those questions?"

"I do." And if being confident meant she did, she did, but I wasn't ready to admit it.

"Haw! Arnie doesn't, and outside of Miss Perry, he's about the smartest one in town."

"Miss Perry? You mean the schoolteacher?"

"Uh huh."

"You figure she's the smartest one in town?"

"Yup."

"Well, do you know Miss Perry believes just exactly the way Uncle Julius believes?"

That was a stopper.

"No, I don't."

"Well, she does. She was here last night asking Uncle Julius if he'd be willing to visit her classes this fall. Afterwards we talked about Christ. Anyway, you should know what she believes. She teaches a Sunday school class in your church."

I was losing the argument, I knew. "Well, I can't see it."

"It's not that you can't, you don't want to."

"Don't need to."

"Oh, yes you do! You're a thief. You're a liar."

That got under my skin, "I am not!"

She ignored me. "You're a lot of other bad things, too, and if you don't accept the Lord Jesus Christ as your Saviour, you're going straight to hell."

I have to admit it, hearing her say a word like that jarred me, I was that shocked. There she was in the fading light, sort of pretty and sweet-looking, innocent, and a girl at that, and yet I heard her say it.

"That's no language for a girl to use. If your papa heard you say that he'd likely give you a paddling, big as you are."

"Oh, no he wouldn't! It's the truth, whether you want to admit it or not. You have stolen things and you have lied, but you have a bigger sin than that."

"I do not!"

"Yes, you do."

"No, I don't!"

"Yes, you do."

"What is it?"

"Unbelief, and unbelief is the only sin that will send you to hell."

"Aw—I don't know."

Her tone changed, "I'd be afraid not to believe."

"I'm not," I said, but that was a whopping big lie and I knew it. Memory had a way of proving a thing like that.

She went on, sort of dreamy-like, and maybe even forgetting I was there. "I'd be afraid of dying if the Lord weren't with me. My mother died in January. I was with her. She knew she was going to die, and just the day before she told me, 'Rachel, this will be harder on you than on me. I have no fear, for though I must walk through the valley of the shadow of death, Christ will be with me. I'm sorry to leave you, honey, but this is the way the Lord wants it.'"

Rachel stopped talking for a minute. The sun was so far down I couldn't see her tears, but they were there. "Mother said other things, too, then she went to sleep and the next morning she was gone."

"I don't plan on dying real soon." Why I said a thing like that I wouldn't know.

Rachel never let on she heard me because she went on talking, "It was Uncle Julius who introduced Mother to the Lord before I was born. Mother's the one who introduced me to the Lord, and after the funeral I talked to Daddy, and although Uncle Julius and Mother had talked to him lots of times, it wasn't until we were alone in the house and everybody else had left he said he had to have help. The Lord helped him, too."

"I've gotten along for a heap of years and haven't done so bad."

Rachel fell into silence and so did I, and that kind of silence took the starch out of anything I had to say, so for a change I didn't play the part of a fool but kept my mouth shut.

The crickets were plenty noisy, along with frogs, and away way off, Dusky was whippoorwilling for all he was worth.

The moon was out, soft and creamy, and the trees reflected shadows on the surface of the pond. What with the squares of light coming from the windows at the mill it was nice, though at the moment, sad and pensive.

It wasn't long before Mr. Wade called from the porch, "Rachel, come in, and bring Jerry along for a glass of iced tea."

It was surprising to hear him call me by name, and pleasing, too, but I was in for a bigger surprise when I entered the mill. Everything was old-fashioned, even the electric lights were made from old lanterns. Round, braided rugs were scattered here, there and everywhere on the oak floor; bright, cheery and colorful as the ones Mama made, only heaps bigger. The one in the middle was eighteen feet across at least.

That living room was a whopper, fifty feet long and forty wide, and none of it was dead space, so to speak. One corner looked like an old-fashioned lawyer's office, bookcase filled with leatherbound volumes, rolltop desk eight feet long and six feet high, and I might say that desk was considerably cluttered. There was another desk, smaller and just as cluttered near it. There were two swivel chairs, one occupied by a tall, middle-aged man, black-haired, wearing a white shirt open at the collar, and a necktie pulled loose for comfort. Mr. Wade's basset hound was asleep under a pine table.

The stone walls were decorated with pictures: paintings, and photographs framed in pine, and hanging from wooden pegs. I suppose I could go on almost an hour telling about the pictures and the different pieces of furniture, and not even get around to mentioning the piano and harp, or the cage—a whopping big one twelve feet long and eight feet wide with about twenty canaries perched on the limbs of a tree, a live one, mind you, in the middle of it.

The strange man turned out to be Rachel's dad, Mr. Kell. He gave me a look that bored clean through as he said,

"Hello, young man," brisk and sharp and turned to his work again. I could see he was going through a stack of photographs.

Rachel explained, "Uncle Julius has just completed a manuscript for a new history book and Daddy is getting it ready for the publisher."

Mr. Wade came out of the kitchen with a tray of iced tea and cookies. We sat down and finished them off in no time. Mr. Wade poked a few friendly questions at me and I figured he would go after me the way he did Arnie, but he didn't. He said to Rachel, "I think Jerry would like to hear you play the violin."

She didn't say no, or have to be begged at all, but got up and dug a violin case from behind the piano and tuned it up, giving the piano keys a bang and then twanging the strings until they matched. When things suited her, she tucked the violin under her chin and started to play.

I didn't recognize the songs but they sure were something. That Rachel girl seemed to be part of the instrument and like as not, she forgot we were there because sometimes her eyes would close. I'd never seen anything like that before—I mean a barefoot girl with a trace of mud on her ankles, in a yellow dress playing an instrument that made a fellow awful restless deep inside and sort of sad, sadder even than I was when we were at the pond. It's a funny thing, this kind of sadness was sort of nice rather than discomforting.

Her father never missed a lick of his work, but you could tell he was listening, and Mr. Wade was listening, too, eyes closed, head resting on the back of the rocker, and going to and fro in rhythm with the music. The canaries also were in on it and now and then one or two would burst out into song that fit right in with the music.

I'll tell you, before the evening was over I found out that Rachel girl was full of music. She banged a lively piece off on the piano, then went to the harp. And that was something to hear, but it was nothing like the violin for getting at a person's feelings.

After Rachel finished we had another round of iced tea

and some more cookies. Suddenly I noticed the clock over the fireplace that said eleven-thirty and I got up startled and gulped, "I'd better be getting along."

Mr. Wade jumped up too and exclaimed, "I had no idea it was this late!" He reached into his shirt pocket and pulled out a pamphlet. "Here, Jerry, when you get a chance, read this."

"Yes, sir," I mumbled and headed for the door.

The walk home wasn't like any walk I had ever had before. It was as though I had been away for a year and had to get reacquainted with the old things again, and I might say, when I entered our kitchen I got acquainted with Mama right off.

"Do you know what time it is, Jerry? Do you know I've been sitting here worrying for two hours, wondering if something happened to you?"

"I'm sorry, Mama. I just didn't know how late it was."

"The next time you go fishing I want you home at nine-thirty."

I didn't bother to explain what had happened, but climbed the stairs and went to bed.

Sleep came easy, but it didn't stay long. I woke up dreaming, or nightmaring, as you might say. It seemed I was in a coffin and couldn't get out. It was so dark it seemed to press in on me.

I suppose I was only half awake when something touched my shoulder and all in one movement I jumped, crashed into the wall and fell off the bed and onto the floor.

"Jerry, whatever ails you?" It was Mama. She snapped on the light and I got up chagrined, to say the least.

"I never heard such mumbling in your sleep, Jerry. What ails you?"

"Nothin'. I just had a nightmare."

Mama fixed the bed up, patting my pillow so it was fluffy, turned out the light and returned to her room. I eased my door shut, turned on the light and dug the pamphlet Mr. Wade had given me from my pants pocket. It was like the one he had given Arnie entitled, "Seven Presuppositions." I'll tell you something, after reading that, it was hard not to believe in Christ and yet, I fought it, but didn't know why.

I sat on the edge of the bed and stared at the pamphlet and thought of what Rachel had said, and thought to myself, "You dope! You're scared lily-white and when John Kordick catches you it will be your end. And what are you doing? Sitting here stubborn." But no matter how hard I tried something inside of me wouldn't let me ask the Lord for help.

I snapped off the light, got in bed, pulled the sheet over my head and when that didn't help, added the pillow, but that didn't blot out my troublesome thinking, either, so I tossed and I turned, and I guess I dozed, because the next thing I knew Mama was sitting on my bed. "Whatever is the trouble, Jerry?"

"Plagued nightmares," I mumbled.

"It's almost too hot to sleep," Mama said. "Why, you're soaking wet! Jerry, something is troubling you. Don't you want to tell me what it is?"

"Mama," I blurted, "do you believe there's a God?"

"Why, yes!" Mama said, startled-like. "Don't you?"

"I don't know," and there that rebellion was in me again.

Mama sat there in the dark for a few minutes before she spoke again. When she did, she didn't sound especially happy. "If that's what's troubling you, Jerry, I guess I'm at fault. I've seen to it you've gotten the proper food, had your teeth checked, your eyes examined, and we've seen you've gotten your education, and I guess I've taken care of just about everything except that question."

"It's all right, Mama," I said. "It's just that I got to dreaming about some crazy things."

Mama didn't ask me what I dreamed about, nor did she say much of anything. She just sat there for half an hour and finally kissed my cheek and went off to bed. I knew she was sad and I wondered what she believed, because she never said much about it, and I never did hear Papa say anything much about what he believed. I dropped off to sleep from sheer exhaustion and not because I had any peace.

The next day turned out to be a dilly. I went to work at twelve and wasn't there ten minutes when George Hostler walked into the store.

I hadn't seen him since he had been fired and had heard he had left town, but there he was as big as life, and with an awesome looking scar on his right cheek. All at once I knew where he got that scar. It hadn't been Joe on the roof that night. It hadn't been Kordick. It had been George. I didn't know how he managed to get by Rusty, because Rusty hated him, but I knew it had been George.

I was staring at him when he turned my way. "What's the matter with you?" he growled. "Pokin' yer nose in somebody else's business again?"

"Nothin'," I mumbled and turned to my work.

He asked Arnie, "I hear there's a rumor around town."

"Town's never rid of them," Arnie countered.

"Lucy's been telling me, since I've been gone that Kordick thinks I run off with his old woman."

I perked up my ears. This was news.

"I heard it this morning," Arnie said, "and I do understand Kordick's looking for you. He claims after you were fired from McCormicks'—"

"I quit!" George roared.

"Quit or fired," Arnie went on, "you went up to Kordick's and John wasn't home."

"Yeah, I stopped by to see if he had any need for a hired man."

"That's not what Kordick believes. He's got the idea fixed in his mind that you were courting Millie on the sly."

"The fool!"

"Well, if I were you," Arnie said, "I'd avoid John."

"Avoid him, nothin'. I've already sent word to him if he wants to see me, I'll be sittin' in front of Lucy's place at one o'clock, eatin' lunch. That is, if my credit's good with you and you'll let me have a loaf of bread and some bologna. I'm broke. Been huntin' all around for a job, but they're hard to come by."

Arnie said, "What do you want, rye or white?"

"Rye."

"Plain bologna or summer bologna?"

"Summer."

Arnie put the items on the counter and said, "Now make up your sandwich and then I advise you to hit the road. Nothing good can come of you meeting Kordick."

"Nothing much good ever came my way. Here, gimme your knife so I can cut this bread." George slashed the loaf from end to end and laid the bologna between the halves, left the store and went across the street and sat down among the other men.

Arnie was disgusted and said so. "It's a town of idiots." He no more than had his shoes off, when on they went again, "Well, here it is."

I looked up to see Kordick walking toward George. I tailed after Arnie as he left the store and by the time we crossed the street the men, filled with crusty banter, warmly excited and anxious, had gotten off the benches and formed a circle.

George was still munching his sandwich and we got there in time to hear him say, "You're about the biggest fool I ever saw, Kordick, and if you think you can bluff me, think again."

"I ain't bluffin', Hostler." Kordick started toward George. George stood up, turned his back, pulled a dirty handkerchief from his pocket, carefully wrapped the remainder of the sandwich and laid it on the bench, wiped his hands on his trousers and slowly turned to face Kordick.

Kordick was a third bigger than George, at least. George bounced on his toes a couple of times, cocked his fists, "I've been itching for this." He danced in and walloped Kordick flush on the nose and backed off, with Kordick following apelike, a matchstick hanging from his lips.

In came George again and his fist rammed John's nose. Kordick didn't raise his hands, but held them loosely at his side, half open. He hunched forward and plodded after George who bounced around as nimble as a billy goat, now and then darting in and clipping John. Hostler drove the matchstick into John's lip on the fifth blow.

John stopped and spit the broken matchstick and some blood on the ground, then went after George again.

The two men were breathing heavily; George high and gaspy, and John low and wheezy. Blood trickled from John's lips and nose and his left eye was considerably reddened. He hadn't swung at George once. George continued to dart in time after time and you could hear the thud of his blows. It looked like he would win the fight hands down.

Kordick hesitated. George darted in. Suddenly Kordick's left hand came up and grabbed George's shirt just below the neck. George swung away with both fists, but there was no stopping Kordick. He drew his right fist back and drove it flush into George's face, not once, but time after time with an awful sickening kind of sound. I don't think George knew anything after the first blow, but he couldn't go down. John held him up by the shirt.

Blood spurted from George's mouth, nose, and from a gash across his right eye.

Suddenly John kneed George in the pit of the stomach. A terrifying explosion of breath burst from George's mouth.

Someone shouted and I recognized Arnie's voice. He entered the circle of men and tried to push his way between the two, grabbing Kordick's fists with both hands. "All right!" he shouted, "You've done enough."

Kordick pushed Arnie away, knocking his hat off, and again smashed George, who was now limper than a feed sack. Arnie hauled off and brought his right hand around and slapped Kordick's cheek, making a sound like a rifle shot.

Kordick released his hold on George and stepped backwards on Arnie's hat. The stiff straw made a crackling sound as it collapsed. George went down in a heap.

I thought John was going to turn on Arnie, but he didn't. He looked at him, looked down at George, and spit with about as much contempt as I had ever seen, then walked away, blood pouring down his face and George's blood staining his left sleeve and hand.

Arnie said, "Some of you fellows better get water to bring him around," then he added, "if you can."

Arnie headed back to the store but I hung around while they propped George up on the bench with his back against the tree and brought three buckets of water and drenched him. His eyes opened and it must have been fifteen minutes more before he said anything. He spit out a mouthful of blood and mumbled, "Where's my sandwich?"

Somebody handed it to him. He unfolded the handkerchief from around the bread and patted his face, took a couple of deep breaths and asked, "How did he look?"

"Bloody as you are," someone laughed.

"I'll get him for this for certain sure. I'll get him for this." The next thing I knew he was eating his sandwich.

I figured I was in for a bawling out when I returned to the store, but I was wrong.

CHAPTER 13

"Run over to my house and ask Clarisse for another hat. There's an old one in the cellar way. If she happens to ask, just say the one I had is worn out," Arnie said.

I was back in twenty minutes. Arnie was sitting where I had left him. A couple of people were in the store going over the details of the fight. Arnie wasn't saying anything and I noticed his face was an odd pink, almost like the color of his feet.

I was busy for the next hour, for Arnie didn't wait on any of the customers and he still wasn't saying much.

At quarter to six there were no customers in the store and he said, "Lock the door, Jerry, and pull the shades."

This was a job I had never done before; I mean locking up that way. The store was cast in a sickly gloom.

"How come you're closing up?" I asked.

Arnie was hunched forward against the counter, bare feet hooked on the lower rung of the stool, and while I watched he swayed to the right. His mouth was open so wide the gold fillings in his teeth were plain to see. Without a word he toppled over with the same kind of sound a hundred-pound sack of flour would make. The stool went over with him.

He rolled over on his back, crushing his hat beneath him. His arms were extended a little above his shoulders, and if his face were an odd color before it was sickly now: purplish and sweaty.

I knelt beside him and heard him struggling for breath. He stirred and murmured, "Jerry." His voice was thick and fuzzy. His right hand rose up and came to rest on his chest. "Jerry, put my shoes on 'fore somebody—" His voice trailed off.

Putting his shoes on was a task. His flesh was icy cold, and I had to lift his whole leg to do the job. Before I was done I figured Arnie was dead. His eyes were open, but he wasn't seeing anything.

A gasp, like a dry sob escaped his lips and it was a relief to know he was alive.

I was about ready to go for help when his eyes seemed to focus. "Put up the stool, son," he whispered.

I picked the stool up and placed it near the counter.

"Now help me sit."

"You'd better stay where you are. You're sick."

"No." The voice was more a groan than a word. His right hand moved over and held his left arm above the elbow. His face was twisted out of shape and I almost could feel the pain he was having.

His eyes closed and I guess ten minutes went by before he opened them again. "It's not so bad now," he breathed. "Now give me a hand."

It took some doing, but I managed and Arnie sat on the stool and leaned forward on the counter, his head in his hands. "You're not to mention a word about this." Between each word he sucked in air.

"Can't I get help, Arnie?"

"You're all I need, Jerry. You call your mama and just say I want you to do some extra work. Tell her you won't be home until after dark."

When I had hung up the phone Arnie said, "When I'm rested a bit here, I'm going to ask you to break a law. Not a serious one. You know how to drive?"

"Yes, I've driven McCormick's truck a lot."

"You'll drive me home then. We'll wait 'til it's dark. The way I feel I'd never make it. Now you fix yourself something to eat. Just let me alone for a while."

I didn't feel much like eating, but I made myself a Swiss cheese sandwich on rye and drank a bottle of pop.

Arnie didn't stir an inch until Clarence put the lights on on his gas pumps across the street.

"All right, son. You bring the car around to the back door. The keys are in the cash register."

There wasn't anything to driving the car, but getting Arnie into it was about the whoppingest task I'd ever had. He seemed to be without strength and every breath was a chore. No one saw us as we drove to his house.

"You get Clarisse to help you."

Mrs. Beard was an ample woman and a recluse, you might say. In all the time I had worked for Arnie, she had never once been in the store that I knew of. I never saw her with other people and the only time I'd ever seen her outdoors was when she was fussing in the garden.

I went to the door and the second she saw me she said, "Oh, Arnie!" as though she expected something to be wrong.

"He's took sick," I explained. "I'll need your help to get him into the house."

She flew to the car with me. "Dear, dear, Arnie!" she breathed. "It's happened, hasn't it? I knew it would."

"I had a little heat fit, think nothing of it. A night's rest and I'll be all right."

We managed to help Arnie into the house and he sank into an overstuffed chair.

It was a nice room, kind of gaudy with heaps of paper flowers, colorful vases and china animals stuck on nicknack racks, and lots of frills on the couch and chair covers, and lots of little pillows, I might add.

Clarisse took Arnie's shoes off while she talked. "I knew it was coming. A man can't work from dawn 'til midnight for over fifty years and keep going forever."

I reached home about ten and hurried through my chores. I was having a glass of milk and a piece of toast when the phone rang. Mama answered it and called to me. "It's for you."

"Jerry, this is Clarisse Beard. Arnie wants you to come to the house in the morning, get the keys and open up. He's finally admitted he's too tuckered out to think of working tomorrow."

"All right," I said.

Mama was a little curious about the call. I simply said, "Arnie wants me to start work at six," and that satisfied her.

I was at their house at five to six and Clarisse gave me the keys. "He's been awake all night," she said. "He just fell asleep about twenty minutes ago. He said do the best you can, but don't say anything about him being sick."

By the time I opened the store there were three men waiting to buy the makings for their lunches. Then the bread man came.

"Where's Arnie?"

"Not here."

"How many loaves does he want, did he leave word?"

This was something I hadn't counted on, I mean ordering, but I came up with an answer that turned out to be a good one and I used it all through the day. I said, "Same as usual."

Around nine-thirty there was a little lull and I unlocked the drawer under the counter and pulled out Arnie's ledger. I'll tell you something, that ledger was a sight to see and as interesting as a pirate's diary.

I think everybody in town was listed, and all but about perhaps fifteen were in debt to Arnie. Miss Perry wasn't, but Gus was for five cents for a candy bar, and looking at the date showed me Gus couldn't have been more than fifteen when he had bought it.

There were the names of dead people and it was downright amazing to see how much Arnie was owed that he would never get from them.

Elmo Flanders, who died three years before, a crotchety old man who lived alone, owed Arnie $1,002.02. And there were others, but that was the biggest debt owed by a dead person, and it looked to me like Arnie had supported him for about the last ten years of his life.

Some of the living people busted that record, though. Jack Spears, for instance, had run up over $1,300.00, and after going through that ledger between customers, I wondered how Arnie stayed in business.

I guess it was around eleven when I stuck the ledger back into the drawer and locked it, and it was a good thing I did, too, because Mrs. Spears came in, gave me her order, and after it was filled she said, "Put it on the bill."

"I'm sorry, but the ledger's locked up, so it will have to be cash."

She didn't like it. "Where's Arnie?"

"Not here."

"Just wait 'til I see him." She fussed some, but I stuck to it.

"Well, let me take the groceries home now and I'll come back later and pay."

I was downright determined now. "Cash."

Out she stormed, but fifteen minutes later she was back with the cash.

By the time the end of the day came I had gotten cash for every sale, which was probably a record, and it wasn't easy. A lot of people were fired up, but none left without their order and most of them threatened to give Arnie a piece of their mind.

I might say there was a heap of curiosity about Arnie's not being there, and a lot of speculation, too. A number of people were pretty close to right.

Fat Lucy said, "I know that Arnie's sick. You don't have to lie."

"I just said he wasn't here, which isn't lying. He isn't."

"Is he sick?"

"He's not here."

"He's sick. I've knowed it for a long time. Now you tell me, Jerry Berry."

"There's the phone. Call up, if you choose."

I was relieved when she didn't.

It was nip and tuck all day with curious people asking questions, waiting on more customers than I ever thought Arnie had, ordering and keeping stock on the shelves.

I locked up at six and went to Arnie's house. He was

160

sitting in the living room, pinkish-colored and tired-looking, and we went over the day's events.

"You want me in the morning?"

"No. You come in at twelve."

"Oh, Arnie!" His wife was almost crying, "Please!"

Arnie said lightly, "I've been married to that store all my life. Be ashamed to leave her now."

I didn't bother to tell Arnie I was supposed to be off Thursday afternoon and Friday to help with the wedding. I did break my word with Arnie because I shared the secret with Papa and he agreed I shouldn't mention it to Arnie.

On Thursday morning Roger was there and we worked to get the place in shape, trimming hedges, hanging lanterns, edging flower gardens, borrowing benches and tables because the reception dinner was to be outdoors.

The wedding was set for five o'clock and relatives were coming from all over, and Mama estimated that there would be at least two hundred from Papa's side, Mama's side, and Roger's side and they would all have to be put up somewhere for sleeping.

On Friday Roger brought up a truckload of cots he had borrowed from the Salvation Army in Newark and set them up in the barn and the basement, and when we ran out of space took the rest over to McCormick's and set them up in the barn there.

On Thursday I had gone to the store at twelve and Arnie seemed to be maybe a little redder and a little slower moving, but otherwise normal. On Friday he was about the same. When I left a little after six I found a heap of folks had already arrived, with more arriving all the time. Before bedtime came there must have been fifty. It was a regular family reunion.

Saturday was some day! It began with a fight.

Mama sent me over to McCormick's to count the number of cots because she wanted to make sure there was sleeping space for everyone and extra people had come. Joe was there and we got to talking about George and the fight and I said, "Remember I told you about the man on the roof?"

"Yeah." He acted disinterested.

"I know who it was."

"Yeah." He still acted disinterested, which wasn't like Joe at all and I looked at him. His face was sort of flushed and he wasn't looking at me.

"I know who it was," I repeated. "It was that hired man of yours, George Hostler."

Joe wasn't looking at me. "Aw, go on!"

"I know it was. Whoever was up there got pretty well cut up, from the amount of blood he left, and George didn't show up for a while afterwards. When I saw him he had quite a scar. It adds up. Then in the store he warned me about playing tricks."

"Aw, go on."

"It's right, Joe. He knows we pulled that trick on him, don't think he doesn't. And he was up on the roof to lick me for my part in it. Hasn't he tried to get back at you?"

"Naw."

"Have you seen him?"

"Naw." But the way Joe said it wasn't too convincing.

"That surprises me some. There's one thing that surprises me more. The night George was up on my roof Rusty didn't bark. You know that Rusty's the best watchdog hereabouts."

"Aw, go on."

By this time Joe was just plain fidgety, and him saying, "Aw, go on," didn't make sense, saying it when he did and how he did.

I kept on going. "That night Lillie called Rusty and he didn't come right off, and that was uncommon, because Rusty generally stays pretty close to home, 'specially at night."

"Aw, go on!"

I got it then. "Joe, you know something? You know all this, don't you?"

"Naw."

"You're lyin'! I know what happened. You're the only one in the whole world who could come around our place at night without Rusty barking."

The more the truth dawned on me the worse I felt. "You came and got Rusty and took him away, didn't you?" I was shouting now. "You wanted George to lick me. After it was all over you let Rusty go, didn't you?"

"Naw."

I hit him then and he swung back, but not too determined. I rushed at him and he went down without much of a struggle. I thumped him a couple of times. He started to holler, "Jerry, wait! He made me."

I was sick. I didn't even feel like beating him up, I was that disgusted.

"You—my friend!" I said sarcastically.

Joe was bawling. "He found the cardboard, Jerry, honest. And he figured out what happened and he lay out behind the barn for me. He caught me and he threatened all kinds of things. He threatened to burn down the house and the barn if I didn't tell him what happened—" His voice trailed off.

"So you blamed me!" I screamed.

"He wasn't going to do much, just lick ya."

"And you didn't admit to your part of it at all?"

"He said he'd burn down the barn."

"You dirty rat! You dirty rat! You double crosser! If I ever see you anywhere near our place again—" I was lost for words. "You just wait! I'm finished with you forever!"

Joe got to his feet, brushing off his clothes, not looking at me. "If he'd ever found out I had anything to do with it, he'd beat me up!" Joe whined.

I lit into him again but it wasn't much of a fight and I gave it up and walked home. I'll tell you, I'd been down in my life a heap of times, but I figured I couldn't go much further down than I was then.

I avoided the mob of people around the house and went off in the woods with Rusty and when we were far enough away I got down on my knees, put my arms around his neck and for the first time since that night, talked to him nice, and all the time I was bawling.

I went back to the house around twelve and told Mom

how many cots there were. She was so excited she had clean forgotten she had asked me to count them, and put me to work right off, and that's what I was kept doing until four o'clock when Mama said, "Go change your clothes, Jerry. We've only got an hour."

Changing a fellow's clothes doesn't sound like much of a job, but it was. People were everywhere: cousins, nephews, nieces, uncles, aunts and people I didn't know and I couldn't get in the bathroom at all. My room was cluttered up with bags and coats and girls combing their hair in front of the mirror.

I finally took my good clothes, snatched a washcloth from the closet, went to the brook and washed and changed in the woods.

I returned in time to join the mob of people in front of the house.

Pastor Wallace was standing with Roger and three of Roger's boyfriends as stiff as statues, looking toward the house as though they expected to see it explode. Miss Perry, who was the organist at the church, was playing a portable organ on the front porch.

Suddenly the front door opened and out came three girls, friends of Lillie's, dressed about as colorfully as butterflies, with flowers in their hands. They paraded across the lawn as stately as princesses.

Betsy came next, decked out in pink, and sort of looking like a flower, which I guess was the idea. In one hand she had a big basket filled with flower petals. She dug down into it and had a gay time tossing those petals every which way as she walked toward Pastor Wallace.

The organ music changed and Miss Perry jumped into the bridal chorus. Papa and Lillie came out the front door. It sounded like about all the women in the crowd thought they were looking at an angel, for they ooohed and aaaahed considerably.

Papa had a funny expression on his face, like he wanted to laugh and cry at the same time, and with him dressed the way he was I could understand why. He sort of looked like an

164

over-sized cricket, considering the tails of the coat and everything.

Lillie was different, I mean, she didn't seem like my sister at all. I never thought much of the dress that Mama and she had been working on until now, but I had to admit it was something; long, white, with a piece of cloth trailing out behind for maybe ten feet, and held up by two little three-year-old nieces, and they weren't doing much of a job as far as I could see, but having a gay time of it.

It took Papa and Lillie a long time before they reached the rest of the people, and there was some mumbling and Papa walked away and took his place beside Mama, and Lillie took Roger's arm.

From the porch a lady I didn't know started to sing. The song was pretty, but sad I thought, and dolefully slow, something about "I Love You Truly."

When she finished I could hear Pastor Wallace, but I couldn't hear what he said. I saw Roger's and Lillie's lips moving from time to time, but I couldn't hear them. The next thing I knew one of the girls was helping Lillie lift her veil and Roger was kissing her, and Pastor Wallace shouted, "And now I present Mr. and Mrs. Roger Whitcomb."

Miss Perry really went to town on the organ then and Mama and Papa and Roger's parents and the bridal party lined up and folks crowded around shaking hands with a lot of laughing and kissing.

All around it was a pretty lively evening, with a heap of talk, and I noticed more than one man go out behind the barn, so I sneaked back and found quite a group of our relatives and men I didn't know, and I supposed they were from Roger's family, passing bottles around. I figured if Mama knew what was going on she'd have put a stop to it.

It was getting pretty dusky when Papa got hold of me and said, "Get Joe and a couple of the other boys and light the lanterns."

I didn't bother getting Joe, whom I saw now and then nursing a black eye, but I got some of my relatives and we got the job done in short order.

There was no question about Lillie's plan to light up the lawn being a good one because it turned out downright beautiful and 'most everybody said so.

Along about this time Pastor Wallace stood on a chair and banged two pans together until everybody was quiet. "Dinner's just about ready," he announced, "and Adam Ross has requested me to ask the Lord's blessing on the food. Shall we bow our heads."

After the blessing was over people filed by the tables and served themselves from heaping plates of all kinds of food; you name it and it was there. I guess the relatives on both sides of the family had tried to outdo each other in bringing different kinds of food, and they succeeded.

We started at one end where we got a tray, paper plate, silverware and paper cup. There was one thing Lillie hadn't figured on, that was what those lights would do for the bugs for about one hundred miles around. It was something to see: moths, beetles, mosquitoes, and about every bug in the world was represented. It was something to scoop up a spoonful of potato salad and start it for your mouth and have a bug dive into it, and I wasn't the only one who was having that experience, because there were enough bugs to go around and there was a considerable amount of complaining from the men, a lot of squealing from the women and quite a few of us fellows had fun capturing as many as we could in the paper cups.

Around dessert time somebody asked for the bride and groom because there was a big cake and they were supposed to cut it, but Roger and Lillie had skipped out, which seemed like a dirty trick, considering all the trouble everybody had gone to. But they weren't there, and that was that.

I could tell a lot more about that wedding, but I guess it wouldn't help the story much, especially the part where some of the men behind the barn got to singing some rowdy songs and how their wives were humiliated no end and tried to put a stop to it and couldn't do it, and gave up in tears.

If I'm any judge that wedding started off a couple of family feuds and maybe even a couple of love affairs, from what I saw, but all in all it was a gay time and it must've been two o'clock before Papa and I went around turning out the lanterns, much to the disappointment of maybe two or three billion flying things. I might add there were some beauties among those moths, some as big as the palm of your hand, and others not much larger than pinheads.

"Well, it's over," Papa breathed when he turned out the last lantern.

"How come Roger and Lillie ran off before they got to cut the cake?"

"Roger's wisdom, I would say. I'm afraid some of the friends and relatives had some uncouth plans that Roger didn't want any part of." I didn't know what he meant, but I didn't bother to ask, being as tired as I was. I went up to bed. At least I went up to my room, but I didn't go to bed. There were six little boys tucked in there, and I ended up sleeping in the hayloft without a blanket. While it was itchy, it was private, although as sleepy as I was I had trouble dropping off because I got to thinking about Joe McCormick and the trick he'd pulled.

CHAPTER 14

SUNDAY WAS just as brassy hot as the week had been and as the day wore on the wedding guests left. At noon about forty ate dinner with us and about half of them headed for home afterwards.

Papa got hold of me. "Jerry," he said, "I've paid for this whole thing and I might as well pay for cleaning up. The place is a shambles. See what you can do."

The place was a shambles. I don't suppose one out of ten paper plates had been thrown in the baskets we had put around to use for waste and garbage. The same with napkins, and if anything, the paper cups had a worse average. At first I picked the debris up with my hands, but then I got smart and sharpened a stick and speared them and emptied the spear in a burlap bag. Mama's flower beds were done for; tramped flat except for the rose bushes which had a way of protecting themselves.

Mama was concerned about the silverware, and she had every right to be. It was borrowed from the church: 300 forks, 300 knives, 300 spoons.

I had already picked up some and now that I set my mind to it I found more, and in the oddest places. A knife was in a wren house, tucked in the hole along with a spoon. A fork was jammed in a tree with the tines bent beyond repair. I worked the count up to 291 knives, 287 forks, with the spoons coming in a poor third, with only 254 showing up by suppertime.

Mama said, "I'll have to go to Newark and replace them from the five and ten."

The lawn had been poorly because of the dry hot spell, but if it was poor before, it was downright sick now with parts of it worn down to nothing but dust, especially where the tables had been.

There were only a few people for supper that evening and they left at dusk. Betsy, irritable from lack of sleep, was put to bed amid tears and later Mama and Papa sat on the rockers on the front porch while I sat on the steps.

"Well, it's over," Papa sighed.

"I wonder where they are now," Mama said.

"Somewhere between here and Maine."

"Probably in Connecticut some place."

"Lillie—married. It's hard to believe."

"She's a woman now," Mama said, which was a little ridiculous, I thought, but I didn't say anything, figuring Lillie was only a day older than before she was married.

"Yes," Papa said in agreement, "but it's what she was made for. I often thought about it and never believed I could accept it, but I have."

"Roger's a good boy; a man, I mean."

That conversation was a puzzler and when there was a lull I put in, "Roger will probably bring her back if Lillie takes off on him the way she did on me. Just wait 'til he finds out."

Mama laughed, "I guess I forgot you were there, Jerry, but the Lillie you saw was not the Lillie Roger saw."

"Just wait 'til he finds out," I insisted. "Bossy, brassy, over-neat."

Papa interrupted, "You figure Lillie was the thorn in your flesh, but Jerry, I'll tell you something, you were ten times more a thorn in hers: a torment, a tease, and sometimes downright repulsive."

"Huh?"

"That's right, downright repulsive. You don't know it, but Lillie is extremely feminine, and your approach to life—worms for fishing, mice and snakes for pets, barn smells and general lack of cleanliness—was something she couldn't understand."

I couldn't see it and the whole conversation seemed out of my range, so when the mosquitoes increased their business for the night I went up to my room, leaving Papa and Mama mostly satisfied, but a little sad, rocking away on the porch.

I'd been asleep for a while and when I woke up I could still hear the comfortable murmur of their voices and the occasional slap of their hands on their cheeks or arms. I dropped off again, thinking of how good it was not to have Lillie around, and yet a little doubtful about the thought.

I worked around the house in the morning because there was still a lot of cleaning up to be done. Papa was off to Trenton and Mama was quiet, while Betsy moped around asking about every two minutes where Lillie was, with Mama answering, "Lillie's married now, honey."

"When's she comin' home?"

"In two weeks, and then Roger and Lillie will visit us and then they will go to their house in Brookfield to live."

But the answer didn't reach Betsy and she kept right on asking where Lillie was.

I was glad when Arnie called up at eleven and asked me to come to work.

Arnie didn't look good. I'll go further, he looked sickly and said so. "I'm tuckered, Jerry, and you can give me a hand. If it's all right with you you can count on coming in when I open up in the morning and staying until I close at night. It's too much for me, and without you here Saturday I just about gave out."

George Hostler came in about twelve-thirty with his face showing the results of the fight. "I'm bummin' again. Looked for work, can't find it and if I'm gonna live, gotta eat. How about stakin' me to a week's grub? Someday I might pay you back."

"It's against my better judgment," Arnie said wearily. "Jerry, fix up a bag of stuff we can't sell."

That wasn't hard to do: two stale loaves of bread, a pie that had been dropped, some fruit slightly tarnished, a dented can of salmon, some dried beans that had spilled on the floor, and three hot dogs flattened when the ice man dropped fifty pounds of ice on them, plus some broken cookies, a sickly head of cabbage and other odds and ends.

Arnie said bluntly, "Consider it a gift. I couldn't sell it anyway. So if you intended to cheat me you can do it with a clear conscience."

George laughed without mirth. "I'da cheated ya, depend on it. I'm movin' out of town. I'll likely never bother to come back. I got just one or two little items to straighten out, and one's Kordick. I owe him something and I'll go to his place tonight and pay the debt off. Never like to leave town without being even."

He transferred the groceries into a burlap bag and hoisted it on his shoulder. "G'bye, Beard, and thanks." He turned to me. "You'da gotten yours, too, kid, and I guess I owe you somethin', but I can't pay it direct, seein' as how you know. But maybe I can pay your old man back tonight."

"He's in Trenton," I said, feeling squeamish.

"Fine. It'll be easier to pay him then. Maybe I can pay your old man back for having a sneakin' son like you."

He left, with Arnie staring after him. "Poor boob, never could tolerate that man. If I'm not mistaken no one's ever cottoned to him. He'll keep right on bumming around the way he has been for the last six years. What's he got it in for you for?"

"I don't know," I said, lying, and the subject was dropped, but I was bothered and I wasn't too interested in having him tell Mama what I'd done, but there was nothing I could do about it.

I stuck close to home that evening, not going up to see Rachel like I'd planned to. I mean, not going up to the pond like I wanted to. I kept looking for George, but he didn't show up, and I went to bed relieved.

About twelve o'clock I was awakened by the clang of the fire gong in front of Clarence's gas station. The town was divided up into five sections and you could tell in what section the fire was by listening to the number of gongs: one for the center of town, two for the west, three for the south, four for the east and five for the north. The one handling the hammer was striking the steel gong four times, pausing and then four times again.

East was our section, so I was alerted. I climbed out of bed, on to the roof and saw a little glow in the sky. First I thought it was McCormick's. So I dressed and hustled over, making Rusty stay home, although he didn't like the idea and wanted to come.

I was wrong, for McCormick's place was safe, but Kordick's barn wasn't, and by the time I arrived it was going good. A horse and two cows had been led out and were tied to a tree near the house. The volunteers were there and the fire engine was pumping water on the blaze, but getting nowhere, for the dry spell, plus the old wood and tons and tons of hay were too far gone to save.

After a while the men quit pumping the water because there was no use and they stood off watching, just keeping an eye on the house and the other outbuildings to prevent the fire from spreading.

Kordick was there barefoot, standing a little closer than the others, until the heat drove him back.

Somebody called, "Got an idea how it started, John?"

"Yup," he growled, "George Hostler."

"You sure?"

"Yup." He pulled a piece of paper—the paper I'd wrapped the hot dogs in that afternoon—from his pocket and showed it to the men. "I found this on my doorstep when I came out of the house."

People crowded around and I did, too, and saw written on the paper in crude letters, "We are even. G. HOSTLER."

Kordick called George some filthy names that I won't mention, saying, "I heard this pounding on the back door, pulled on my pants, come downstairs, turned on the kitchen light and found this paper slid underneath. I opened the door and that's when I seen the fire. I'll get 'im, you'll see!"

A thought hit me; slammed into me. This was the debt George owed and he owed it to me too. I flew home. The lights were on all over the house and when I entered the kitchen Mama was holding Betsy in her arms.

"Whose place was it?"

"John Kordick's barn."

"I'm glad you've come home. I've never heard Rusty carry on the way he did. I went in your room to get you and you were gone. Then I saw the fire. Rusty barked, carried on something awful and I must've called him a hundred times but he wouldn't come."

I remembered then that Rusty hadn't greeted me when I came home. I went to the kitchen door and called. I heard him coming from behind the barn. He stopped at the bottom of the kitchen steps, looked back into the darkness to the south, growled, came up the stairs, tongue hanging out, panting, and aquiver with excitement.

I knew what had happened. I knelt down, put my arms around his neck and almost choked him with a hug. Mama didn't know and I never let on. She passed his barking off by saying, "I guess he knew there was a fire and didn't like it."

The glow from Kordick's place softened and soon died out completely. Then came a lonely wail of a single blow from the fire gong telling everyone it was all over.

I didn't know whether George would come back or not, but with Rusty on the job, good old faithful Rusty, I figured that if he did he'd get an unwelcome welcome.

Everybody talked about the fire when they came into the store the next day. It was some surprising to find people softer toward Kordick and feeling downright sorry for him. That, I might say, was not a feeling I shared, but I figured when a man was disliked more than Kordick he would have to be pretty low, and I had to admit George Hostler met the requirements.

Arnie was doing poorly; not getting off the stool but maybe once or twice during the day. It's a funny thing how Arnie had changed. He stopped bellowing at me, even when I dropped a crate of eggs and broke about half of them. He'd say things, too, that were things I had never heard from him before, like, "I sorta wish you were my son, Jerry. It would solve a lot of problems right now." That was one I couldn't understand. "You're a good worker, Jerry; steady and dependable," or, "You got a good mind, Jerry, just don't waste it. I wasted mine." But the most surprising thing he said was, "Julius likes you, Jerry. He's a brilliant man. If I were you, I'd stick close to him. Don't make a bore of yourself, but you listen to him. Ask him about education. Take his advice. Find out what university he thinks you ought to go to."

I'd never thought much of anything past high school and it surprised me to hear Arnie say, "Miss Perry's high on you, Jerry. She said you were one of the brightest students she has had." That pleased me and it set me to thinking seriously.

Gus came into the store and said, "The state police have been notified about Hostler. I don't think they'll ever find him. He's likely had a life full of adventures like this one. He knows how to keep out of sight."

"You figure he's gone?" I asked.

"Gone for good, and good riddance," which was a relief to hear but I kept looking for him anyway, just in case.

John Kordick was still a problem. He was drinking heavily and his search for the person who tricked him and had run off with Millie had become an obsession. He had blamed George for a while, but a report drifted back to town about two weeks after the fire that George had been seen tramping along the road near Wilkes Barre, Pennsylvania. "George wouldn't be walking if he had that money," John told Gus, "so it weren't him."

So John was set off again looking for me; not knowing it was me he was looking for.

On the third Thursday night of August I headed for Wade's place, outfitted with a can of worms and my pole. I broke from the brush and saw Rachel on the porch with Julius Wade. She was a sight to see, dressed in white with her dark hair loose, but perfect you might say, and with shoes on fancy enough to be worn at a wedding. I had broken from the brush and without knowing why, swung around and plunged into it again.

Rachel had seen me and called, "Jerry!"

I broke out again, trying to look surprised at her call,

trying to cover up the feeling I had inside of me at seeing her.

Mr. Wade said, "Rachel, why don't you teach Jerry how to use my fly rod."

Rachel went into the house and came out barefooted, but still dressed fit to go to church, carrying two rods. She handed one to me. It was surprising to feel how light it was. It was longer than I expected and at first clumsy.

It looked so easy watching Rachel arch that feathered bug to just about any place she wanted to put it, but it wasn't easy.

Suddenly Rachel put her rod down and stood beside me. "Easy does it," she whispered. "Let your wrist do most of the work. Raise the rod straight up. Strip out more line."

I didn't want to take her advice, but I took it, even though it hurt.

"Don't hunch over so! Not sideways. Too fast, Jerry, too fast! Up, straight up. You're snapping it too hard. Easy does it."

Suddenly I got the rhythm of the thing and the bass bug dropped gently on the water.

"Oh, that was good!" Rachel talked like it was her own victory and she clapped her hands.

I didn't say a thing for twenty minutes and she kept whispering, talking all the time. She nursed me into getting that feathered bug as far out as she had done, and further.

It was a curious thing to see the sun go down and the moonlight take its place, and about as beautiful as a body could stand. The rod became part of me and the bass bug sailed with grace.

I wasn't thinking of fish. I was thinking of how nice it was to please her. The bug touched the water and formed soft circling ripples in the dim evening light.

There was a volcaniclike explosion of water. The line snapped straight. "Not hard! Not hard!" Rachel said. "Just hold him tight. That's only a four-pound leader, it can break."

That fish did some surprising things, and it's funny how sensitive that rod was.

"When he rushes away from you, strip out line," Rachel said.

I did. That was some bass. He threw himself out of the water time after time. He plunged to the bottom of the pond. He rushed left, then right.

Lights sprang on in the house and our shadows fell on the dark surface of the pond. It was something to feel; I mean, to know the bass was out there somewhere like a dog trying to break from a leash, and I sorta felt sorry for him, but not enough to want to lose him.

Seven minutes passed, ten, fifteen, maybe twenty, and they were about as lively a group of minutes a fellow could put together with Rachel whispering all the time. The whispering wasn't needed anymore for I sensed what I was supposed to do, but I can tell you one thing, I didn't bother to tell her, not wanting to break the spell.

The fish tired and I drew the line in. "Now is the time to be careful," Rachel breathed. "Lead him gently—gently—gently—that's it. Oooh, there he is. Slide him in."

The fish was tummy up, his mouth wide open. I leaned over as his nose touched the shore, and I hooked a finger under his gills and raised him up. I had never seen a fish so large before. It was downright pleasurable to hear Rachel say, "I never caught a bass near so big! Come, let's weigh him."

I pulled the hook from the bass' mouth and we headed for the house. Rachel didn't stop at the door to wipe the mud from her feet, nor did I.

Mr. Wade exploded, "Well, now, that's a fish! That's a fish!"

Rachel ran to the kitchen and returned with the scales. I hooked the fish's gills on the scale and Rachel read, "Six pounds, nine ounces."

I couldn't help myself and I started talking, "Now isn't that something! Now isn't that something! I wouldn't have believed it. I didn't believe it. How can a little rod like that catch a fish like this? I'm sorry I teased you. It shows what

176

kind of a fool I was." I said other things, too. I don't think any of them were too bright.

Mr. Wade broke in. "Jerry, you hustle home with your fish. Change your clothes and come back. I'm having guests in a little while and we'd like to have you join us."

You can guess I hustled and I got a lot more pleasure when Mama saw the fish. I laughed some when she said, "Six pounds, nine ounces—why that's the exact weight of Betsy when she was born."

I shifted into my Sunday clothes, telling Mama why, and it wasn't long before I was picking my moonlit way toward Wade's again.

That fish had been a shocker, but entering Julius Wade's home brought another shocker, for Arnie and Clarisse were there. Clarisse was some overdressed, like maybe little-girlish, but Arnie was the sight, looking downright funny without his straw hat and with a necktie on. I looked at his feet. He had low shoes on and his ankles were puffed out above the tops and I can say this, Arnie just didn't look good.

And there's something else, too. Arnie was different, and as Rachel's dad, Mr. Wade and Arnie talked, it wasn't long before I discovered Arnie was doing a heap more agree-ing than arguing. It didn't take me long to find out the reason. He was just adding to what he already believed. I mean, he was just looking for more information on some-thing he knew about. I mean, it seemed to me Arnie must have said to Mr. Wade somewhere along the line, "I know Christ as my Savior," and now he was as much as saying, "I need a heap more information to dig into this thing deeper," and Mr. Wade was entering right into the thing and giving that information a heap faster than I could understand.

Clarisse was listening, docile and yet interested, and it might seem a silly thing to say, but it was as though she were saying, "Oh, Arnie, make yourself happy," and I think Arnie was doing it, too, because once he said, "I'm tasting this now. It's sweet, that's what it is. It's sweet-tasting to my mind." He laughed sort of odd-like. "Julius, I've got an appetite; you're going to have to feed me." He sort of groaned, "When a man's played the part of a fool for so many years, he faces a lot of regrets. And when a man's been hit," he touched his chest, "he has to learn fast."

That was an interesting conversation even though about 90 percent drifted over my head. After a while Mr. Kell left the circle and with Rachel's help set the table. When it was done we were called to it.

It's a curious thing; I had sold Mr. Wade the Swiss cheese, the ham, the pickles and the heap of other things. When I sold them they were just things, but seeing them on the table was startling and a thought that was away beyond me touched me. Something like—it's a curious thing how common things can become so uncommon when uncommon people touch them. The conversation around that table was easygoing.

After the refreshments were over Rachel and I went out on the porch. Rachel said, "Let's take off our shoes and walk on the grass."

That turned out to be a good idea and we walked around the pond listening to the night noises and having the moonlight glinting through the trees and the stars as bright as I had ever seen them.

We perched on the tree trunk, dangled our feet and splashed the water, sending out ripples of silver. Moonlight's funny stuff, it's not like dull sunlight, or dawn light, or dusk light. It's a light of its own. I don't think there is anything like moonlight for making a body feel or see uncommon things.

Rachel must have noticed it, for she breathed, "It's like an enchanted world!"

I was feeling downright happy. "Rachel," I said, in a quavery old man's voice, "See them there stars up in the sky, and see that there moon? I'm gonna tell you how they got there. Once upon a time over in Larimer's Valley—that's four hoots and two hollers from here—there was a crotchety old man, Tyrus Quiggle, by name, who had a billy goat. That billy goat was one hundred seven years old when Tyrus decided to butcher him. You can guess a goat that old would be plenty tough, and he was, so Tyrus built a hot fire to tenderize that carcass. He built the biggest fire a body ever saw and he kept it going for near a week with the billy goat roasting on a stick. Now and then Tyrus would haul off and test the meat, but that billy goat was still tough.

"It was a Tuesday night, midnight. Tyrus tested the meat again. It was tougher than agate, so he hauls off and kicks the fire with his hobnail boot in disgust. Sparks went tearing everywhere. They went sky-high as you can plainly see for looking. That there moon is the biggest spark and them there stars are the little sparks."

Rachel laughed and then sobered right off. "Jerry, men have sillier ideas than that explaining how those things came to be, but I'm sure glad I know how they really began. The Lord created them."

It's funny how I didn't like Rachel saying that. It seemed like every time the Lord was mentioned it was worrisome, and just the mention of the Lord set me to thinking. My mood changed. The night noises filled the silence for a couple of minutes. "Jerry, you told me once that Arnie Beard was the smartest man in town. I guess you know he has heart trouble."

"He's been sick," I said.

"I heard him tell Uncle Julius how he did some serious thinking when he was feeling bad. He couldn't come up with any decent answers to his secret questions at all. He talked to Uncle Julius, and Jerry, I heard Arnie Beard say, 'I believe Christ is the only answer.'"

I had had a hint of that conversation in the house. That made me even sadder, somehow. I mean, knowing that Arnie had done it.

"Wouldn't it be nice to know that all your sins were forgiven?" Rachel asked.

My thoughts ran wild. I looked at myself in a way I had never looked at myself before. Talk about sins; mine flicked through my head like figures going on a cash register. I was a liar, an expert one. My thinking took a different turn. I thought of Arnie having heart trouble. If it hadn't been for me he probably wouldn't have had that attack after George and

John fought. *Bang!* another one hit me. I had tricked John and sent him to drinking. *Bang!* another one. I had been the cause of George Hostler's problems. *Bang!* I'd really been the instigator of the fight with Joe McCormick. *Bang!* I'd been the one who helped Millie run off from her husband. *Bang!* I'd been the one who gave Gus the chance to be mean. There's no use telling all that went through my mind, but it was enough to shake me, and I knew if Papa found out, as big as I was, he'd take a switch to me.

I got to thinking the Lord knew all about them. There would have to be an awful big licking waiting for me at the Judgment Day. For the first time in my life I was afraid of the Lord—I mean terrified.

I can't tell you what went on inside of me. All I know is I said, "Come into my heart, Lord Jesus." I'd heard that invitation I suppose a hundred times in Sunday school, in church, in the tracts Mr. Wade gave Arnie and the one he'd given me, but it was the first time I had ever used it personally.

I did an awful dumb thing right off. I cried. I mean, I cried. I forgot Rachel was there. At least, I forgot until she said, "That's good, Jerry, that's good."

I pulled out of my private thinking, "What's good?"

"You just told me you accepted Christ as your Saviour."

I didn't remember saying it out loud, but I didn't bother to tell Rachel. I simply said, "A body can pile up a heap of bad things in a little spell if he sets his mind to it, and it 'pears to me like I've set my mind to it lately."

Before I knew it I was telling Rachel about everything; I mean, about Kordick and Hostler and the whole works.

Doing what I did sure did something inside of me, I mean, I felt clean—cleaner and brighter than I ever had before, but with problems. That Rachel girl saw to that. "Jerry," she said softly, "what are you going to do about those things?"

"What do you mean?"

"It's true God has forgiven you because Christ died for

you, but Arnie hasn't forgiven you, nor has George, nor John Kordick. You're going to have to ask them to forgive you."

I could only think of John Kordick at the moment. "You mean you expect me to march up to John Kordick and haul off and say, 'Mr. Kordick, I'm the one who tricked you. Forgive me'?"

Rachel laughed, but I didn't see anything funny about it. "I think that's what you have to do," she said.

"Nosiree!" And I was never more positive of anything I had ever said. I was that positive for about thirty seconds, then I knew Rachel was right.

We didn't talk too much after that. When Mr. Wade called us the spell was broken. We slid from the trunk of the tree into the water, up to our knees. I don't know how it happened, but somehow my hand touched Rachel's, and if catching the bass was something, this was double that. I deliberately moved close to Rachel as we were walking toward the squares of light at the house. The back of my hand touched the back of her hand again and she didn't pull away and I can't tell you what was going through me, it's that far beyond words.

I didn't say anything, nor did she. I grabbed my shoes and socks from the porch and I tore off through the woods toward home, running like a deer with so much strength I figured it wouldn't have been too hard to jump up and touch the moon with my fingertips.

A couple of days later Papa came into the store about three o'clock in the afternoon. Arnie was on his stool and he didn't bother to put his shoes on.

"Adam," Arnie said, "drag a stool from the back of the store there. Sit beside me."

Papa said, "You have me curious, Arnie. What did you want to see me about?"

Papa got the stool and sat next to Arnie. "I'm tuckered, Adam. I've known for a couple of years something was wrong with my heart. I finally broke down and went to a doctor. He claims I'm on the brink."

"Amy and I have been concerned," Papa said, which

181

was true. I had heard them fretting about Arnie lots of times.

Arnie went on, "When a man doesn't have a son to take over he's in a bad way. I could sell the store easily enough, but I don't want to do that. I mean, I don't want to sell it to just anybody. There's a way I want it run, and Adam, I think you could do it."

You can guess how surprising this was to me, and even more so, when Arnie said, "I've borrowed Jerry as my son. He's been a good boy. In a couple of years he'll be off to college—" Arnie paused and looked at Papa. "Adam, you've been on the road an awful long time. I figure you wouldn't mind being close to your family."

I thought Papa was going to fall apart. His voice was trembly. He looked pale, but by six o'clock Papa was about the happiest man in the world, for he and Arnie had worked out a plan that had them both nodding their heads in agreement. And if you think Papa was happy, you should have heard Mama. She laughed, she cried, she squealed, she kissed Papa, she kissed me.

"Jerry, Jerry, why you're the cause of all this." I had to admit I felt good about it myself.

But I didn't feel good later that night when I thought of going to Kordick and asking for forgiveness. I argued with myself and came up with a hundred reasons against doing it. I knew Kordick had cheated me. I knew he was mean to Millie. I knew he had stolen her money. Those facts were prime arguments against doing anything. I also knew, plain as day, that his wrongs didn't make my wrongs right. I knew I had to go to him.

So the next day at noon I told Arnie, "I'll be back in an hour," and walked toward Kordick's place; praying, you might say, for the first time, for help.

I got to thinking about what I had said about being back in an hour. That, I figured, was an unlikely prophecy, for I was heading straight into all of Kordick's threats. I'll tell you one thing, it was hard for me to walk down that road toward Kordick's. I stopped once and got to thinking about dying and how he would do it: with a knife, with a gun, with a rope, or maybe an ax.

"Well, Lord," I murmured, "I have to do it. Maybe I'll see You in a few minutes. It's sure better, I mean, I feel better, knowing You. It's not like it would have been before. I'm glad of that, at least."

I didn't have much comfort and only a wee smidgen of hope as I plodded on, going slower and slower until a snail would have passed me hands down, until I got to his house.

John was behind the house sitting on a crate, working on an inner tube that was already patched so often it would have looked comical if I hadn't had my problem. Beyond was the black scar of the burned barn, with the leaves on the trees nearby hanging dead from the amount of heat they took. John's dark shirt was darker because of the sweat and the closer I got the more I smelled the raw whiskey on his breath.

I jammed my hands into my pockets and walked to about six feet from him. He was grunting like an animal as he worked.

"Mr. Kordick."

He looked up with dull eyes.

"I've come to tell you I put the scarecrow in front of your house and I helped Millie get to the bus."

"Huh?"

"I ask your forgiveness, Mr. Kordick."

"Huh?"

"I did mean things to you."

"What do you want, boy?"

"Mr. Kordick, I'm the one who tricked you. I stole Jack Spear's scarecrow and put it in your yard. I helped Millie take the twenty thousand dollars to the bus when she ran off."

John turned to the tire. "Don't plague me, boy. Don't plague me."

"Mr. Kordick, would you forgive me?"

"Don't plague me, boy. I'm busy. Can't you see?"

What could I do? I backed off and returned to the store, leaving John messing with the inner tube in a dull sort of way.

Papa was there and I couldn't keep my mind on what he and Arnie were saying, for thinking of John and whether or not he understood me.

It was about three o'clock when Arnie stood up and took Papa's arm, he was that weak and wobbly he could barely stand alone. "Jerry," he said, "come here." He took my hand. "I'm going home, son. I can't go on any longer. It's your father's store now." He looked around at the shelves, the counter, at the icebox, and his eyes filled with tears. An explosion of breath left him. "All right, Adam, take me home before I make a bigger fool of myself," and he was gone, and the store was never emptier.

Ten minutes went by. Clarence came over, bought a box of cough drops and said in his slow poky way, "Hey, Jerry, I'm gonna be best man at Gus and Jane's wedding, how about that?"

That caught me off guard. I stared at Clarence, not believing, yet having to believe that it was true. I was sorry about that, but what could I do about it?

He left and John Kordick came. I'll tell you something. At a time like that I found it easy praying, even though I didn't know much about praying. Kordick was wild-looking. "Where's Arnie?"

"G-gone home." I was stuttering.

"What you said back there," he jerked a thumb toward his house, "did you tell Arnie that?"

"No, sir."

"Your papa?"

"No, sir."

"Anybody?"

I was about to lie, but lying was out for me. I was tired of doing that anymore. I sucked in my breath. "I told a girl, Rachel Kell, that's all."

"Didn't tell Lucy?"

"No."

"You're sure you done them things?"

"I did them, just like I said."

"Took by a dirty, shirttailed kid." He didn't say it mad,

he said it sort of in shock. "You done it because I cheated you out of the five dollars?"

"Mous— I mean, Millie paid me the five dollars."

"Hostler wasn't in on it?"

"No."

"Did he know about it?"

"No."

"Took by a dirty shirttailed kid!" he roared. "Where did Millie go?"

"Mr. Kordick, I promised Millie I wouldn't tell anybody, and I'm not going to. I'm done lying. I'm not going to tell you."

"Probably went off with one of the boys," John said dully. "You ain't told nobody else. Nobody else knows?"

"No, sir."

"You planning to tell anybody else?"

"Arnie and Papa."

He looked at me, his moist lips rolling the match back and forth. "Anybody else?"

"George Hostler if I ever catch up with him."

Kordick lunged and grabbed my shirt and lifted me clean off the floor. "Do you know where Hostler is?"

"No," the word was choked out of me.

He slapped my face. "You're not tellin' Hostler."

"I tricked him, too." My words were squeaky. "I have to tell him, same as I told you."

Kordick released his grip. "He's gone. You promise me you won't go looking for him. I don't want him knowing. Promise?"

"I won't look for him," I said weakly.

"I oughta kill you, but I thought it was a man. You're just a dirty, shirttailed kid." He bawled out in a wail, "You're nothin' but a dirty, shirttailed kid!"

John went out the door straight for Lucy's place.

I was that sick I sat on the stool, but I felt clean, real clean, and I thanked the Lord for that feeling, too.

Papa came back and hitched an apron around his waist. "Ross and Son, how does that sound, Jerry?"

"You mean for the name of the store? I guess all right."

"No, that won't do. We'll keep it Beard's." He ran his hand through my hair. "I'm a happy man, Jerry." He frowned. "Our gain is Arnie's loss, but with a little rest I think he'll perk up. Whoops, here comes our first customer."

I saw Jack Spears pulling up in front of the store in his junker. I didn't bother to tell Papa Clarence had been over, since Papa seemed to date taking over the store with Arnie's going, but I did say to Papa, "Papa, let's make it cash-and-carry, 'specially with Jack Spears."

"Right, partner," Papa said with a grin. So we were in business together and that was a good feeling.

I took off the following Monday afternoon at three and headed for Rachel's. We fished, but things weren't lively so we sat on the porch and talked.

Rachel was most sad. I thought maybe she was upset with me for something. "What's the matter?" I asked.

"It's been a happy summer; a nice one," she paused.

I added, "A warm summer."

"Jerry, I'm going back to New York tomorrow." There are not many words in that statement but I don't think I ever heard words that shook me as much as they did.

"Tomorrow," I said dumbly.

"We're leaving at five in the morning."

Julius Wade poked his head out the door. "All right, you two, come on in. Supper's ready."

I followed Rachel into the house and there were a stack of suitcases and boxes near the door, looking for all the world, and making me feel like, they were tombstones.

That supper didn't suit me, it was that sad; not that it was talked about, it wasn't. Well, how can a fellow explain a thing like that? Rachel and I did the dishes together and by the time we were finished it was dark outside. You could sense fall in the air; not that it was cold, but there was a different tune the insects sang, and the smells were different, too.

We went down and took our shoes and socks off and climbed out on the tree trunk, not saying much.

Then I started to talk, telling Rachel about Kordick and

about how the store belonged to Papa, how glad Mama was, and how the summer had changed so many things, and how instead of just figuring on getting out of high school I was figuring college now and a heap of other things. "And, I'm thanking you, Rachel, for—how did you put it? introducing me to Christ. Your Uncle Julius may have had a hand in it, but you were the clincher."

I don't know why, but if there was ever a night of wanting to cry, that was it; with Rachel talking about her music, about New York, and there was a lot about the Lord Jesus sprinkled between all she said.

Rachel taught me a verse, too, and I memorized it with just a couple of stars peeking through the clouds overhead. I knew then I'd never forget that verse. "And we know that all things work together for good to them that love God, to them who are the called according to his purpose."

I guess it was about ten o'clock or maybe ten-thirty when Mr. Kell called out, "Rachel, we'd better get to bed. We have a long drive in the morning."

We carried our shoes and socks to the house. I said good-bye to Mr. Kell and headed for the door.

"Mr. Kell," I asked, "could Rachel walk with me to the edge of the clearing?"

He nodded and we left the house together. I deliberately moved close to Rachel. I reached over and took her hand in mine. She didn't pull away and that's a feeling I could never forget.

"I'm awful sorry you're going," was all I said, until we reached the edge of the clearing. I learned something then. I learned a body can do things without knowing what he's doing or at least, not planning on doing the things he's doing. I dropped Rachel's hand and I put my hands on her shoulders. I could see her looking at me in the pale glow coming from the house. I kissed her ever so lightly on the cheek. "Good-bye, Rachel."

She tiptoed and kissed me, whispering, "Good-bye, Jerry."

I know I couldn't have stayed there any longer without

crying, so I headed for the woods and after going about maybe a hundred yards I shouted, "Good-bye, Rachel!"

Her voice drifted back, "Good-bye, Jerry!"

I didn't go any further. I sprawled on the damp earth. I leaned back and listened to the night noises around me. I must have been there an hour thinking, thinking about a raft of things: some past, some present, but most future. It was all bittersweet, or sweet-bitter, with happiness and heartbreak so mixed together a body couldn't untangle them.

Suddenly something touched my face; a wet, moist something. I grabbed in the darkness and found it was Rusty. I hugged him some, scrambled to my feet and we backtracked to Wade's place. The old mill was dark. A wind stirred the trees and rippled the pond. I turned with Rusty following me and moved toward home.